Vigil and Other Stories

Derek Mortimer

Vigil and Other Stories

Vigil and Other Stories
ISBN 978 1 76041 738 3
Copyright © text Derek Mortimer 2019
Cover photo: David Monje via Stocksnap

First published 2019 by
GINNINDERRA PRESS
PO Box 3461 Port Adelaide 5015
www.ginninderrapress.com.au

Contents

Vigil

Alison stands on the edge of the station platform shivering and looking hopefully along the lines of shining steel tracks that emerge from the tunnel. Torrential rain has fallen all weekend, causing washouts and train delays.

A voluminous bag slung over her shoulder contains a book. The current one is Tolstoy's *Anna Karenina*, a story that will occupy her for the rest of the day, the rest of the week, the rest of the month, if she doesn't rush it – maybe even for the rest of her life.

Trains are problematic for Alison. She cannot look at the tracks without wanting to scream. She turns her back. The man next to her is impatiently gritting his teeth beneath his shaved head. He has black shoes, black socks, black suit and black shirt. He looks like a funeral parlour director – except for a yellow tie, which hangs from his neck like a dead budgie. She thinks it's a statement of some sort, 'I am *me*.'

Alison walks slowly up and down the platform among the fretful commuters. The government has promised more trains, next year. Or is it the year after?

Anna Karenina swings heavy in the bag and bumps against Alison's hip; half a million words rubbing one against the other, a flawed heroine, trapped by love. Alison has already chosen her next book, *War and Peace*, another half a million Tolstoyan words.

There are more epics on the list to carry her through the future: one and a quarter million words from Proust's *In Search of Lost Time*; a million from Xavier Herbert's *Poor Fellow My Country*. The days with Mark are long. She has already read a dozen books of similar length in the last year.

The train arrives, eventually. The doors slide open and everyone presses forward. Alison uses her considerable weight to push her way to the second deck. She settles down. *Anna Karenina* lies next to a sandwich, an apple, a litre-and-a-half bottle of sweet orange drink and two large fruit and nut chocolate bars, one for Mark, one for her.

She should have walked. Next time she will, lose some weight. She thinks that every time.

It takes thirty minutes by train, then ten minutes walking. She will be half an hour late. It is hard to know whether Mark will notice.

*

He is propped up in bed, maybe asleep. Maybe not. The bed has been made, the pillows arranged around him.

She asks the Filipino nurse Mary, 'How is he?' She always asks, although she knows what the answer will be.

'Had a good night, didn't you, Mark?' the nurse says.

'Any change?'

Mary nods and smiles gently.

Alison leans over and kisses Mark on his damp forehead above the putty-white scar mass that stretches from one side of his face to the other.

Mark grunts. He scrabbles the sheet aside with what is left of his hands. He grunts again and extends his legs to show her, as though it is her first visit. The flap of skin below each knee is folded neatly over and stitched in a little square where the shins once were. The first time she saw it Alison was horrified by the ordinariness of the surgery, like patches added to something that had worn out.

'It's looking good,' she says. For a moment, Mark's eyes seem to light up. Or is she imagining it?

Alison places *Anna Karenina* on the bed. She sets the bottle of orange drink and the sandwich on the bedside table next to a glass. With a flourish, she produces one of the chocolate bars and holds it out towards Mark. He makes grunting noises from somewhere deep in his chest. Alison peels back the foil wrapping from the chocolate, breaks off a piece and Mark takes it in the stubs of his fingers and pushes it into his mouth.

'You like that?' Alison smiles.

She pours herself a drink of the orange juice, bites off a piece of chocolate and settles her bulky body into a chair next to the bed.

Four television sets facing four beds are disgorging daytime TV. Four different channels, four comatose men in adjacent beds. To try and shut out the babel, Alison puts earplugs in, opens *Anna Karenina* and begins to read: *All happy families resemble one another, each unhappy family is unhappy in its own way.* She puts the book down. Is it true?

Mark is asleep when Mary brings lunch. Alison puts down her book, takes out her earplugs and gently rouses him. She tucks a bib under his chin and slowly spoons soup into his mouth. She carefully catches the stray drops that escape his lips. She wipes his chin.

'There,' she says, when he has finished and the last smear has been dabbed away.

It is thirteen months since it happened. She comes each day, as she promised herself she would.

With the help of Mary, she pulls Mark higher up in the bed and they readjust his pile of pillows. Before it happened, she could not have lifted him. He was the strongest man she had ever known. Making love with him was like making love to a cyclone. He was the best of them all.

Alison reinserts her earplugs to try and block out the chattering TV stations before going back to her reading. Mark gazes at the nearest screen. An interviewer has two party political men in the studio. She puts questions to each of them in turn, trying to find some commitment, some passion, even an answer, but there is none.

Mark would once have roared his disgust. Politics and sex was what had brought them together. Politics was his passion – after women.

Alison found her own way to cope with those other women. Mark sits looking blankly ahead. Perhaps something is registering. Perhaps. The important thing is to be with him. Occasionally a door opens in his mind for a moment, then just as quickly the wind of the past blows it shut. He does know one thing: when she arrives – and when she leaves.

Alison goes back to the ice and snow of imperial Russia, to *Anna Karenina* and her lover, the dashing Count Vronsky; and her cold, imperious husband, Alexis Alexandrovich Karenin. None of the characters is able to hold Alison's attention. She puts the book down on her lap and looks across at Mark. She gets up and pours herself another drink of orange juice and stands, sipping. The sweetness fills her body and soothes her mind. She shouldn't. Her doctor keeps warning her of the consequences for her worsening health. He is right of course and she will stop. But not today.

Mark's head turns slightly in her direction. Alison smiles. There is no response. He reaches for his chocolate, fumbles a piece. She moves to help but he ignores her.

Alison holds up her bag then puts it down again to show that she is going out, but coming back. Mark makes a noise between a grunt and a squeal. Alison smiles at him again.

Outside, she walks along a cracked concrete path that edges a small garden. Grass and other weeds grow in the gaps. High on a gable a currawong calls, then launches itself into the fading glow of the winter evening. She follows its flight with her eyes as it swoops and loops then disappears from sight.

She returns to Mark. He grunts. She strokes the stump of his hand then sits down to read, but her thoughts stray to Tolstoy and his death. Alison looks at Mark. He is asleep. Should she waken him before she leaves, or slip quietly out?

She puts *Anna Karenina* into her bag, leans forward and kisses Mark on the forehead. His eyes open. She lifts her hand, opens and closes it in a butterfly gesture of farewell.

Mark sits up abruptly, eyes wide. He moans and shakes his head.

His cries become louder and he kicks his legs until the bed sheet tumbles to the floor revealing the mutilated limbs with their ridiculous patches.

Alison stills the arms that are waving and pointing to where his legs were. She takes the blunt stumps of his fingers and holds them, hard in her palms. 'I'll see you again tomorrow, I promise.' She releases his hand. 'Try to sleep.'

She turns her back and walks from the room. The sound of his wailing follows her down the corridor. She passes a nurse she hasn't seen before.

'I'll settle him down,' the nurse says.

Alison smiles and hurries on.

*

She sits on the almost empty train. It would be nice to just keep going, an endless loop through the suburbs, and the city, Circular Quay, the harbour, then round again, a bag full of sandwiches and books. She thinks again of Tolstoy's introduction to *Anna Karenina*: *All happy families resemble one another, each unhappy family is unhappy in its own way.* It's true. She knows no one else who is unhappy the way she is.

She can only guess about what is happening in Mark's head.

Alison doesn't go directly home when she gets off the train. She checks her purse to see how much money she has, enough to take herself and *Anna* into a bar close to the station. It is early evening and quiet. She buys a glass of white wine, then finds a corner and sits.

Rereading the book after such a long time is like reconnecting with an old friend years after they have died and remembering their pains and their pleasures. She thinks about *Anna Karenina*'s awful death under the wheels of a train. Self-sacrifice. Punishment. *Punishing.* Trains and death. Tolstoy had a thing about them. In the novel; a shunter is horrifyingly crushed. Tolstoy himself died at Astapovo, a remote railway station where he had gone to escape his nagging wife,

Sophia. But he was an old man by then, it wasn't suicide – or attempted suicide.

Anna was punishing her lover, Vronsky. Her death wasn't the terrible climax of the novel. The climax was the *effect* her death had on Vronsky. She punished him by killing herself.

It hadn't been like that with Mark. He punished *himself*. He felt he had failed his friends, so he jumped under a train. He came out the other side mangled and alive. The ultimate failure, failure to kill yourself.

What would Vronsky have done if Anna had been unsuccessful in her attempt at suicide? Would he have sat by her broken body each day, feeding her, wiping her chin? Taking chocolates to her? Reading to himself? Feeling guilty that he had not foreseen what was coming and prevented it? Or would he have gone off to manly war as he did on her death?

Why hadn't Tolstoy thought of having Anna punish Vronsky by surviving her suicide attempt? Maybe he had.

Anna wanted Vronsky and her husband Karenin to suffer. Mark was not trying to make anyone suffer, but they did – those who took his advice – ultimately Alison's advice. Instead of trying to stop Mark she had encouraged him to dabble in things he knew nothing about. She thought he might even make a quid or two, and if he didn't, he'd have learned something about how the system worked – he did, and so did she. Mark was a scaffolder by day and like her, a passionate political idealist day and night. But he didn't know a good business deal from an elephant trap. Neither, as it turned out did she.

'Just the once and we'll be set.' He'd argued for investing in a 'sure thing', IT dealing, someone had tipped him off about. When it looked like the adventure was going well, he wanted to share his good fortune – and his cleverness – with their friends. That was typically him, sharing good things, and showing off.

She didn't know at the time that he'd withdrawn all his money and invested it. The lot.

Alison drains the last of her wine, sets the glass back on the table. She picks up her bag and *Anna*. They step out into the dark street together and cross the railway bridge to home, comfort for each other in the long night.

Same Time Next Year

'I'll live another year then, Matthew?' I sat on the edge of the examination bed and slipped my T-shirt back on.

Matthew smiled and nodded without looking up. 'Yes, and keep out of the sun.'

'No option. I've stuffed up my shoulders, haven't been in the ocean all year. How's the last twelve months been for you?' I said as I tied up my shoes and stood, ready to leave and catch the train.

I expected the usual response – 'Fine, went to Bali, London, New York, Melbourne, Rome, Wagga Wagga' – that sort of thing, not necessarily all of them, or any of them, but you know what I mean?' A non-response to a non-question.

But Matthew stopped writing and turned to me. 'Not the best, Andrew.' He paused. 'My wife took up with my best mate.'

I didn't know what to say. Usually when you've just had your annual check-up at the skin cancer clinic, and the doctor's zapped the carcinomas, you're relieved, and want to be on your way.

'Chrrrist,' I said. 'It must have been devastating.'

'It was. Never thought it'd happen to me.'

'How did…um…?' I sat down again. 'How did you find out?'

'We were all the best of mates, Peter, his wife Samantha, my wife Melissa and me. For years. Used to socialise all the time, eat out every week, each other's house for dinner, same parties, go on holidays together. Our daughter Anne and their daughters Natasha and Alicia got on great. It was perfect.'

By now he had swung round in his chair and was facing me. 'Samantha and me are smokers and we used to duck out to the deck or the street and leave Melissa and Peter at the table while we had a quick one.'

I don't think he was aware of his double entendre.

'Then one day when Samantha and me were outside ruining our lungs, she said that she thought something was going on between them. Their conversations seemed false, like they'd suddenly changed subjects each time we returned.'

He sighed and smiled. 'I told her she was imagining things. But I watched them over the next few weeks. Everything seemed normal. But Samantha was still suspicious. So one day,' Matthew picked up the mobile phone that was on his desk, 'what I did was, each time we went out for a smoke, I left the phone on the table, with recording on.' He put his phone back down to demonstrate.

'Samantha was right. What they said in front of us and what they said to each other when we weren't there was very different.' Matthew screwed up his mouth at the thought. 'It was the most painful thing I've ever listened to.'

I could imagine. Awful. Absolutely awful.

Matthew sat in silence. I couldn't think of anything else to say. He was my doctor, not my close friend.

After a while, he continued. 'I confronted Melissa. She cried. Said she'd been stupid. That she loved me. That it was finished between her and Peter. An escapade she'd regret the rest of her life. Asked me to forgive her. He said pretty well the same, that he'd betrayed me, his best mate, said he felt ashamed. He'd been under a lot of pressure at work, that sort of nonsense. It was all over. He hoped we could get back to being friends again. I'd covered up for Peter with Samantha so many times when he'd been off with another woman. He was a serial philanderer. I never thought that one day the other woman would be my wife.'

I thought it should have been obvious but I didn't say so.

'Forgiveness. It was a big ask of both Samantha and me,' Matthew said, 'but I love Melissa. It was time for a new beginning. Samantha felt the same. A lot was at stake after all those years – two families, and the rest.' Matthew went quiet.

'So how's it working out?'

He looked up at me. 'Peter often travels interstate with his business, legal stuff, he has pots of money, so he was out of sight if not out of mind. Melissa said she needed her own space till everything settled down. I agreed and we rented a little flat for her. Just for a couple of months, close, so we could see each other whenever we wanted, but be apart while we sorted things out. To be honest, even though I still loved her, it was hard being in the same house, sharing the same bed. I lost twenty kilos in two weeks. We met every few days and talked. And talked. She kept saying she loved me and we had to patch it up. I agreed. Anne kept visiting her. I'd have liked more support from Anne, but that's the way it is. Melissa's her mother no matter what. It was humiliating.' Matthew shook his head. 'Everybody knew.'

I wondered how would you feel? A cuckold. Some guy playing around inside your wife. Others feeling sorry for you, talking about it, hoping it doesn't happen to them, wondering if it is happening to them. I waited for him to continue.

'One night I was really missing her and wanting to talk. I went round to the flat. The lift was leaving just as I got there so I walked up to the third floor. Who should I see going into Melissa's place but Peter, with a bottle of wine in his hand. No doubt a very expensive one. I hammered on the door. Someone looked through the peephole. I hammered again. Eventually Melissa answered. She looked anything but happy, but she opened the door and I went in. Peter appeared from the little kitchen with three glasses clinking in one hand and a bottle in the other. If he was surprised, it didn't show. I coulda killed him.

'"We're talking things through," he said, looking serious.

'"At ten o'clock at night, with a bottle of the best Pinot Grigio?"

'Melissa said, "'It's not what it seems."'

I could picture it, almost a domestic farce.

'You can imagine my response,' Matthew said. 'What is it if it's not what it seems? What's wrong with meeting in a coffee shop, in the middle of the day? Or even dinner! Maybe the four of us together, like old times, reconnecting, eh!

'Melissa said not to get angry and Peter kept saying, "Believe me, it's not what it seems."'

It's amazing how often people use that excuse when something is exactly what it seems, but I didn't say anything, I just nodded.

Some guys would rather die than tell you their wife has been shacking up with their best mate, others obviously need to get it off their chest, again and again and again. I wondered how many people Matthew had told. Usually it would be the patient spilling their heart out to the doctor rather than the other way round.

He went on, 'After catching them out again like that I didn't want to see Melissa any more. She kept ringing and begging me to meet her. I'd had enough.'

I got up to go and make way for the next patient. 'How you feeling now? Have you found someone else?' I asked.

Matthew gave a sort of half smile. 'Well, Samantha and me are seeing each other.'

'Oh.' I tried to hide my surprise.

He knew what I was thinking: had each of them fancied the other's partner all along?

He crinkled his face ruefully. 'Our friends now think the whole thing was a wife swap. But it's not like that. Samantha and me were both being swept away. We clung to each other. What happened to me and Melissa was terrible.' He sat looking up at me.

I stood, halfway between him and the door. Eventually I said, 'I hope it all works out.'

'Me too.'

I went back and shook his hand. 'Same time next year then.'

Matthew smiled. 'Yes, same time next year.'

As I opened the door to leave, he said, 'By the way, I've stopped smoking.'

The Dog

I'm standing with a small dead dog cradled in my arms. I'm watching a video of a Muhammad Ali–Joe Frazier fight, the Thriller in Manila. Ali is winning.

I don't particularly like boxing. I don't particularly like dogs either, but this poor little thing, Mickie, is not, or was not, much more than a puppy. His eyes are open and shiny and he is showing tiny white teeth in a smile. He looks alive. But he is definitely dead. His nose is cold. The tip of his protruding pink tongue is cold. His lips are lined with blue saliva that looks like an old whore's lipstick. He has been poisoned. No doubt about that.

Behind me, the room is full of shouting and crying.

I'm holding Mickie because Denise thrust him into my arms. Then she collapsed by the side of Grace's wheelchair and buried her face in the folds of her mother-in-law's beanbag body and sobbed.

That was ten minutes ago. I'm almost forgotten. I don't want to be here any more but I can't just put the dog down on the table and walk away.

I hear Denise say, 'Poor Mickie. Poor Mickie. He never hurt anyone.'

Ali and Frazier are now well into the fight. They are very much into hurting each other.

'Bloody mongrel. The bloody mongrel,' Grace says over and over. She's not talking dog pedigree. She's talking about the person who poisoned Mickie. She rubs Denise's back and wipes her own eyes.

Lester was the one who wanted to watch the Ali–Frazier fight. He said it wasn't just a fight between two black men to see who was the best heavyweight in the world. It happened in '71, Vietnam and all that. The good guys were for Ali, who was against the war, and for civil rights. The bad guys were for Frazier, pro-war, conservative.

That's what Lester said. But he's missing the fight. He's shouting, not at Ali and Frazier on TV, but at Grace, his mum. 'Denise shouldna let Mickie out!' he yells.

Lester married Denise a year ago when she fell pregnant. I've always wondered how women can *fall* pregnant. Why not, *stand up* pregnant, or *lie down* pregnant, which is far more likely. Whatever, she told him she was pregnant.

'Deadly!' he said at the time. 'I've always wanted kids. That's why I divorced my last wife. She couldn't.'

Denise lifts her head from Grace's lap. She has far more wrinkles than a woman of forty-one should have. 'I can't keep the little fella locked up all the time,' she moans.

'Ya shoulda known that mad bitch would do something,' Lester yells.

'How? How should I?' Denise's mascara isn't waterproof. It's washing down her face like run-off from a coal tip.

'Bloody obvious! She's jealous.'

'Of you?' Denise says derisively.

'It was you who said so!' Lester fires back.

'I didn't think she'd do anything like this.'

'Uh? She kicked the side of your car in. She nicked my mobile. She set fire to the garbage bin. She punches people out in the pub, men and women. She's a junkie. An' you didn't think she'd do anything?' Lester yells.

He's going a bit hard on her, she's just lost her pet dog, a present from him.

I wish someone would take him from me, though. He's only little but he gets heavy after a while. I've driven two hours down here from Sydney in the heat to talk to Grace. I don't want to get involved in Lester and Denise's dog fight.

I think Ali wins the fight, but I can't remember for sure. Lester said it marked a turning point for Ali, who had been on the nose for refusing to fight in Vietnam after converting to Islam. He said why should he go over there to kill his brown-skinned brothers who had never hurt him. He was accused of being a traitor to the United States.

I want to hand Mickie back to Denise and talk to Grace about her latest book. I brought a copy with me and its sitting on top of a mobile air con unit where I laid it when Denise put Mickie into my arms. I've got Buckley's chance of talking to her with all this going on, though. Grace is crying too. Her big black felt hat is pushed back on her head. Her normally beaming round face is as sad as a bloodhound's and shiny with tears and sweat. She keeps mopping herself with a huge blue hankie.

I'm the only one not crying. Until today, I'd only met Mickie once, the day Lester gave him to Denise. I didn't know Mickie enough to bond. And he looks peaceful, even happy, with his little smile. The only giveaway that he's dead are those blue-stained harlot lips. It was a cruel thing to do.

Lester's disappeared into the garage like he's been doing all morning. He'll be back in a few minutes, with a guilty look on his face.

'What ya gonna do about Mickie?' I ask Grace and Denise.

Denise sits up. 'Bury him.' She sniffs.

'You can put him under that peach tree I planted in spring. It's not going well,' Grace suggests.

'He'll be good fertiliser,' Denise adds.

I think she's already moving on from grief.

Lester comes back into the house, letting the heat in with him.

Grace shakes her head at him, like she does every time he returns from the garage.

'We should call the cops, get the bitch that done it,' Denise says.

'No bloody way.' Lester's mouth tightens at the thought.

'The cops wouldn't worry if we'd been poisoned, let alone Mickie,' Grace adds.

Denise finally remembers that I'm still holding Mickie. She comes over and takes him from me. She kneels and gently lays him on the ground in front of the mobile air con unit and adjusts the little red leather collar around his neck. 'The only thing he done wrong was bark a bit,' she says, kissing the wiry nose.

I hope she doesn't pick up some of the blue stuff from his lips.

'That's not why that bitch poisoned him,' Lester says.

I ask how they know for sure that their neighbour did it.

'Who else woulda?' Denise says.

'Do ya remember why I bought Mickie for ya?' Lester asks, turning to Denise.

'Don't go on with that again,' Grace tells him.

Denise ignores Lester's question and strokes Mickie's nose.

'I said do ya remember?' Lester repeats.

'Leave it,' Grace tells him again.

'What if we bury Mickie, have a bit of a ceremony?' I suggest.

'Under the tree, eh?' Grace says to Lester and Denise.

'Some bloody dog'll come and dig him up,' Lester argues.

Denise suggests we put a rock on top to prevent that. Scratch Mickie's name on it. We all agree that's a good idea. Nothing much grows in the garden anyway. Lester goes to the garage to get something to dig with.

'Get a towel from the bathroom to wrap the poor little fella in, will ya, Danny?' Grace asks me.

I bring one in and spread it on the floor. Denise lays Mickie out. She holds back strands of her blonded hair with one hand. With the other she wipes the purple line from his lips with the corner of her T-shirt. Mickie lies there, still smiling, eyes open, like he's observing how we take care of him now that he's dead. It gives me a funny feeling seeing him looking at us.

I push Grace in her wheelchair out in to the back garden. The western Sydney sun hammers down out of a brilliant blue sky. We stop in front of the peach tree. Grace is right, it is struggling. The leaves are brown and curling at the tips. The ends of the branches are dead and brittle. The lawn's almost given up its fight for survival and crackles when you walk on it. On the other side of the wooden fence beyond the storm water drain the treeless park bakes in the heat. Everything's struggling.

Lester eventually appears from the garage carrying a spade and a mattock. He drops them close to the tree. He smells of alcohol. He begins to chop erratically at the hard ground with the mattock. Clumps of clay and tufts of dry grass fly into the air. We step back out of the way.

'Watch the bloody roots. You'll kill the poor tree,' Grace tells him.

Lester keeps on digging. After a while, he straightens, spits through the gap in his front teeth. He takes off his shirt and throws it to his mother. Sweat is running down the muscles and scars of his prison-hardened, black body.

I ask him if he wants a spell but he shakes his head and keeps digging. Denise, Grace and me form a semicircle a couple of metres away from the hole that is growing beside the peach tree.

Mickie is cradled in Denise's arms. The three of us watch Lester. We melt like ice creams in the sun.

Something's happening in the Ali and Frazier fight because I can hear the hysterical calls of the commentator even with the doors closed.

Lester keeps digging and gouging until the hole is shoulder deep. Mickie is only a little dog. I look across at Grace. She mops her round brown face with the blue hankie.

'Lester, mate, I think it's deep enough,' she says.

Lester keeps digging.

Denise steps up to the edge of the hole, carrying Mickie in front of her. 'Lester!'

'Piss off,' he shouts from the hole. He's dropped the mattock and is spading the soil out, grunting each time a load comes up over the edge. Even at that depth, the soil is as dry as the inside of a wood-fired pizza oven.

Grace manoeuvres her wheelchair to the edge of the hole and shouts down at Lester, 'We're burying a little dog, Lester, not a cow.'

Lester stops. No more clods of clay come flying over the side. He pitches the mattock out, then the spade. His hands appear on the side, resting on the crumbling earth, then his forearms. He tries to lever himself out. But he can't.

I step forward, stretch out my hands. We grab each other's wrists and I heave. Lester gets part of the way out then slips back. I think I might have to shovel some of the soil back in to give him a platform to stand on. But he sticks up his hand for me to try again. He grabs my wrists, leans back and starts to walk up the side of the hole. I brace to stop myself pitching head-first in, but he has walked up walls before. He knows what to do. He is out, standing on the rim of a grave big enough for an adult human. The peach tree leans at an angle into the hole.

'Lester. Lester, what the bloody hell you playing at? Come on, son,' Grace says.

Denise offers him his shirt from his mother's lap. He grabs it without speaking, wipes the sweat and grime from his body and stands panting in the heat.

Denise walks over to the hole, slipping and sliding on the dry earth in her thongs. She looks down. 'How'm I gonna put him in?' she asks. 'I can't just drop him.'

Lester grunts. 'I'll find a rope.'

'I'll help,' I tell him. I just want to get out of the sun. We all want to get out of the sun, except maybe Lester. I'm not sure what he wants.

'Nah.' Lester strides off in the direction of the garage.

I look at Grace. She looks at me. I feel like I should start filling the hole in but I don't want to interfere. Not with Lester like this.

Denise has started to cry again. 'It wasn't my fault,' she says.

I don't know whether she's talking to Mickie, Grace, me, Lester – or the peach tree.

'I just wanted everything to be all right,' Denise says. She's still cradling Mickie and standing on the edge of the hole.

It takes Lester five minutes to find a rope and come back. You could tow a truck with it. Somehow, Lester ties a knot around the towel. Denise stretches out her hands. She wants to lower that little bundle into that big hole herself. Lester pushes her hands aside. She starts to sob, the sweat, the mascara, the tears, the wisps of her wet hair, all getting mussed up together.

Lester gently lowers the bundle into the grave. The three of us get as close to the edge as we safely can and watch as it settles on the ground. I hope Denise doesn't want to give it a Christian burial.

Lester flicks the rope to get it clear of the towel. It comes free eventually but it uncovers Mickie. Mickie is still smiling. I'm beginning to think he knows something we don't. But that's a stupid idea.

Lester begins shovelling back the clay. He won't let me help.

When he's done filling in the grave, he returns the rope, the mattock and spade to the garage and doesn't come back.

I wheel Grace into the house and park her in front of the air con unit.

'You know the story of Mickie, don't ya?' she says.

I nod. 'Yeh, Lester bought it for Denise when they got married.'

'Not just that. He bought it because she was pregnant. Then they got married. He was mad for kids of his own. Loved 'em. Couldn't get any with his first wife.'

'Well? That's what I said.'

'Yeah but, Denise wasn't pregnant.'

'The doctor got it wrong? A phantom pregnancy?' I ask.

'Nothing phantom. No pregnancy. At all. Denise wanted a husband as much as Lester wanted a kid.'

'But he was bound to find out.'

'She was gonna claim a miscarriage.'

'And?'

'Lester worked it out. That son of mine's got problems but he's not stupid. They both have problems. But Denise is stupid.'

I don't feel much like talking to Grace any more about her book. I'll leave them to it, come back later.

I get up to go. The TV's still on. I'd forgotten the fight. Ali must have won because he's bouncing up and down, arms in the air in the centre of a mob of people in the ring. Lester's missed it this time. He'll probably watch it again.

I leave Grace sitting in her wheelchair. The book is still on top of the air con unit. I'll be back in a few weeks when things have settled down.

The book's about her life: the family, eight kids, two already dead, Lester in prison ten years. Her people, stolen country, stolen children, stuffed up everything. But because it's written by Grace it's full of hope and humour.

What I want to ask her is how she can still laugh after what she's gone through.

As I climb into the oven that's my car, Denise is in the garden looking down at the pile of clay where Mickie's buried. She has his dog collar in her hand.

A Seat in the Square

The man appeared in the small square late morning. He sat on the seat beneath an ancient plane tree and placed an overnight bag at his feet. He took a phone from his pocket, checked it, pecked out a number and put the phone to his ear. He listened intently before sliding it back into his pocket.

After a short time, he removed a book from the bag and began reading. Every once in a while, he lifted his eyes from the book and looked along the narrow cobbled street that ran down to the lower part of the village.

It was early spring and the plane tree was still unfolding crinkly leaves which provided little shade. There were as yet few tourists but the small pension and café across from the square was open and a couple of tables were set up on the footpath.

After a while, the man left the square, crossed the street and sat at one of the tables from where he could see the tree and the seat beneath, and beyond that the street.

A woman came out of the pension, greeted the man and asked him what he would like to eat. The man was English and spoke no French other than a cheerful '*Bonjour*' and '*Merci*' and '*Oui*'. He nodded and said quietly, 'Good afternoon.'

She was in her mid-fifties, with short-cropped salt and pepper hair, broad hips and a warm smile. The man was a few years older. He took off his hat, revealing longish, wavy hair, flecked with grey. He ordered a beer, and vichyssoise soup. As she prepared the food in the small kitchen, the woman watched him as he sat sipping the cold beer, all the time looking across at the square. He was handsome, in a scholarly way, with rimless glasses and aquiline nose, but also athletic-looking, like someone who gets up early and goes for a run every morning. She thought she had seen him before but could not remember when.

From where he was sitting, the Englishman could see along the street until it disappeared around a corner. Below, the rooftops of the medieval village glistened in the warm midday sun. When the figure of a woman appeared, he strained forward for a better view before sinking back into his seat. The woman reached the square and kept walking. She was a young tourist, probably German, pretty, an early arrival in the summer migration. She nodded as she passed the café and he smiled back, then watched as she continued on her way before disappearing.

He mopped up the remains of his soup with a piece of bread and sat rolling his almost empty beer glass around in from of him, lost in thought but always with his eyes on the street going down the hill towards the bus station.

After a while he rose, paid the proprietress, picked up his bag and walked to the square, where he sat on the seat with his back to the gnarled old tree. He checked his phone, then slid it back into his pocket. He tilted his head and looked up at the network of steel cables supporting the tree's branches which in summer would carry a deep, green canopy. The first swallows and martins had arrived from Africa and were skimming insects out of the high blue sky.

Whenever the proprietress looked out from the café, the Englishman was still in the square. He sat the whole afternoon, reading, checking his phone, and if a woman climbed the hill, he would lower his book and momentarily peer over his glasses, then turn away and begin reading again.

When the sun had gone from the square and a chill was creeping in, he returned the book to the bag and crossed the road to the pension. He asked the proprietress if she had a vacancy and was shown a room facing onto the square. It was small, immaculately clean, and contained a double bed which occupied almost all the space. The Englishman took it. It was then she remembered where she had seen him: he had stayed at the pension for a few days last summer with a much younger woman. Very pretty she was. They had laughed and joked together a lot, full of fun.

The proprietress's husband was visiting his mother in the next village and he would not be back for a couple of days. Having a guest in the building was company for her.

A short time later, the Englishman came down from his room and ordered an omelette and a bottle of red wine. He sat on one of the outside tables, a scarf around his neck, huddled into himself.

The proprietress urged the Englishman to sit inside where it was warmer but he dismissed her concern and stayed with his meal and his wine, forever looking down the hill to the bottom of the village, forever checking his phone.

The proprietress went and stood by his table, smiled and enquired in her hesitant English whether he had liked the meal. He told her it was excellent.

No one else came to eat or drink and the proprietress sat behind the little bar watching her customer outside, sipping his wine and looking down the street, never relaxing. Because it was so quiet, the proprietress decided to take the tables in and close early. She did not want to disturb the Englishman and invited him to sit inside to drink his wine. He shook his head. He got unsteadily to his feet, and set off down the hill towards the bottom of the village.

Later, he plodded back up the hill and went into the silent pension and to his room. The square below seemed lonely at night, the big plane tree stood sentinel, its trunk knobbly in the shadows cast by floodlight. The Englishman at his window could hear a barn owl somewhere on the edge of the village, a plaintive call over the rooftops. He unwound his scarf, slipped off his jacket and shoes and sat on the edge of a bed that was as empty as the square. He was cold and climbed between the sheets. Thinking of tomorrow, he eventually drifted into a sleep troubled by dreams in which he was endlessly trying to complete some obscure task but was unable.

He felt he was awake all night but he must have slept because the sun coming in through the window drew him from his disturbed sleep. He showered in the tiny shower recess that was squeezed into a corner of the bedroom, dressed and went down to the café below. Tables were already in place on the footpath. The Englishman took a seat and said '*Bonjour*' to the proprietress.

She smiled and asked if he had slept well.

The Englishman said he had, although he had been a little cold. She apologised and said that the weather had turned, after a warm spell, and she had not paid enough attention. He smiled in understanding and ordered coffee and a bread roll. While he waited, his eyes were drawn to the square and the cobbled street where the fragile leaves on the highest tips of the tree caught the rays of the early morning sun.

When the Englishman had finished breakfast, he crossed the street into the square with a book in his hand and sat beneath the tree.

His routine was the same as the previous day. He read, he stood every half hour or so and walked around the deserted square a few times, then resumed reading. He occasionally checked his phone.

At lunchtime, he went back to the café. There was a number of people already seated at the tables but the proprietress went immediately to him and took his order for chicken soup. He felt she was paying him special attention, maybe because he had mentioned the fact that he had been cold the night before. He had not meant it as a complaint, rather a comment.

At the end of the meal, she brought him coffee. He thanked her. She hesitated, as though she was going to say something, but she then simply smiled and walked away. He watched her, the sun on her neck, the sway of her hips. She was a pleasant woman, desirable almost.

The Englishman sat in the square all day as before, reading his book, checking his phone and occasionally looking down the street. In the early evening when the sun had disappeared behind the rooftops of the village, he returned to the pension. He was shivering, and the proprietress insisted that he sit inside the café. She brought him a coffee and a Pernod, then poured one for herself. She smiled over the rim of the glass and took a sip before placing the drink on top of the little bar and returning to other customers.

The coffee and the Pernod warmed the Englishman and he sat for a while watching a young couple and an elderly man at an adjacent table who looked and sounded American. He no longer watched the square.

When he had finished his drink, he went to his room, showered and put on a sweater before going back down to the café and taking a seat inside the door. The proprietress sat on the edge of the chair next to him to take his order.

'Salad, *coq au vin*, and, oh, a half bottle of Beaujolais.'

She smiled. '*Excellent.*'

She stood and the Englishman watched the swing of her hips as she walked back to the little kitchen.

He ate his dinner leisurely. As each course was delivered, he smiled at the proprietress and she returned the pleasantry. He finished the meal with a brandy and coffee, then stood. He indicated to the proprietress with his fingers that he was going for a walk and he turned up the hill into the top end of the village.

The cool evening air and exercise following the meal lifted his spirit. He stood admiring the shadows cast by floodlights on an ancient stone church that dominated the landscape like a castle, then he turned back down the road to the pension. The café was by now empty and the proprietress was behind the small bar polishing glasses. The Englishman paused and said goodnight. She smiled back at him without speaking.

In his room he showered, turned on the reading lamp and sat on the edge of the bed. There was a knock on the door. 'Yes!' he called.

The door opened and the proprietress stood there with a duvet over her arms. 'I don't want you to be cold again tonight.' She stepped into the room and with one motion flicked the duvet so that it settled silently and softly over the bed.

'*Merci,*' said the Englishman.

'Ravi.'

He was not sure what she meant but her smile told him that it was something pleasant. They remained facing each other, neither moving.

'Bonne nuit,' she said. She moved to leave but stopped when she reached the door, 'Last year you stayed here. With someone,' she said.

'Yes.'

'I remember how happy you were.'

'Yes.'

She turned back towards the door then closed it without leaving.

They stood in awkward silence. Then he reached forward and drew her towards him. Beneath his fingers he could feel the firmness of her shoulders, the muscles and bones, the warmth of her body through her sweater as she leaned into him. Close-up, her hair was more salt than pepper. He slid his hands down her back to her waist, and lower to roundness.

She placed her hands around him, then pulled his head down onto her neck. His lips brushed her skin. She held him tight. She could hear the quickening of his breath close to her ear and feel the weight of his head.

The Englishman lowered her onto the soft folds of the duvet. She sat facing him as he unzipped her dress. He caught a brief smell of her body as she peeled the dress over her head. He knelt, gazing at the whiteness of her thighs. She drew him to her.

*

As he walked down the cobbled street early next morning, the Englishman passed a man coming the other way who smiled at him and said, *'Bonjour.'*

The Englishman nodded. 'Good morning.'

The man turned in at the café and greeted his wife. She made coffee and they sat together watching the sun on the top of the plane tree in the square.

'Did the Englishman stay here last night?' he asked.

'Yes. Do you remember him from last year?'

'I'm not sure.'

'He was with that very pretty girl. Much younger than him. Remember?'

'I didn't see her.'

'She was not with him this time. He was alone.'

'Ah, I remember now. Yes. He seemed a nice man.'

'He is. Very nice.'

Deep End

It were the hottest day of summer. Probably the hottest day ever, except in Africa.

The tar in the streets were bubbling. You could pull it up wi' your fingers, roll it into a ball an' throw it at somebody. It didn't half hurt if it hit ya. Mam said it were a stupid thing to do and could take somebody's eyes out.

Michael an' me went ta the big swimming pool – like everybody else. We rolled our togs up in our towels and caught the trolleybus into the city, walked across the centre and up the other side to the pool.

We weren't half hot by the time we got there. The queue were right up the hill a mile long. We were never gonna get in. We coulda got sunstroke waiting. Michael said we shoulda gone to the canal instead but that meant getting another bus. Mam's always told us not to because you can catch polio if you swim in the canal. Michael said you can catch polio in the swimming pool as well but he couldn't because he took cod liver oil every day, summer an' winter. I'd rather get polio than take cod liver oil.

Three big kids came an' walked straight to the front of queue. They was right mucky an' rough-looking. I bet they were from White Abbey, 'Shite Abbey,' that's what we called it. Just because they were from there didn't stop everybody yelling at 'em. A little kid sneaked up an' spit on the back of one of 'em then dashed back to his place in the queue. He woulda really copped it if they'd turned round.

We all made so much noise that an attendant came out an' told us ta shurrup. He said if the queue-jumpers didn't go to the back, none of us would get in. We cheered an' booed as the three walked away.

'We'll get ya all when ya cum out!' the carrot-head leader shouted.

It were hot standing in the sun. I were wearing a new T-shirt, blue and white stripes. My arms were burnt an' going red. So were Michael's.

'If you get too much sun, you turn into a black man,' Michael said.

'How do ya know?'

'Dennis at school told me.'

'How does he know?'

'His dad said. He's a sailor. He's been to Africa. He's seen it.'

'It doesn't go black. When you get really burnt, ya can peel off the dead skin an' you're white underneath.'

'His dad's seen it. How would you know?' Michael said.

I belted him on the head with my togs but he just laughed. He's a real pain, our Michael, a real know-all, even though he's younger'n me.

We moved slowly forward in the queue as kids came out of the baths, hair still wet, skin white and shiny, their eyes red, stinking of chlorine.

Eventually we got in. It were lovely and cool walking on the tiles. Michael and me squeezed into the same cubicle to get changed. I chucked Michael's togs out over the door before he had a chance to put 'em on and he stood there covering himself wi' his hands. He's got a really little willy. Mine's bigger.

'Yer a stupid git!' he yelled. He put his towel round his waist and rushed out.

When he came back, he threw my underpants out. They were all wet when I picked 'em up.

A big, baldy attendant shouted at me, 'Any more from you two and yer out!'

We didn't say owt, just went through to the pool looking straight ahead as though baldy weren't there. That always made 'em mad.

It were packed. An' noisy. There were hardly any space in the water. Everybody shouting and screaming and laughing and jumping in and ducking each other and an attendant in white T-shirt and white pants blowing his whistle and it all echoing in the roof way above us.

It were great.

I waded in at the shallow end. Michael did a somersault and made a huge splash. The water were cold after the sun, like when you get into bed in winter. I ducked me head under and blew bubbles. I kept mi eyes open even though they stung. Everywhere there were white legs moving in slow motion.

Michael said we'd see which of us could hold his breath under water for the longest. He ducked first and I counted. He came up spluttering, water streaming off his face.

'Fifty-eight!' I yelled.

'It were seventy,' Michael shouted above the noise.

I grabbed his head and pushed him under and tried ta kneel on his back. 'It's seventy now,' I said when he came up choking.

I pinched me nostrils together and went under. I sank an' tried ta sit on the bottom. Ya can't. Ya just start ta come back up. It were all legs and bodies 'n' feet, 'n' bums 'n' bubbles, 'n' silence down there. I couldn't hear the shouting nor nothing. I counted.

A girl swam passed me like a mermaid. She looked me straight in the face and blew bubbles. She nearly made me lose count. I'd got up to twenty-seven. I had to beat Michael.

Thirty-five. It were hurting. The mermaid girl came again and blew more bubbles. I bet she'd been up for air.

It were really hurting. Me lungs were gonna bust. I could see Michael's legs. They were bent at the shins and were bluey white.

Forty-five. I didn't think I could do it. I let a bit of air out.

Fifty. I was gonna bust. I was gonna drown if I didn't go up.

Fifty-three fifty-four fifty-five-six-seven fifty-eight-nine sixty. I shot to the surface before I died.

'Forty!' Michael said.

It took forever to get me breath back. 'Liar! It's sixty,' I gasped.

Michael just laughed and pushed me under again. When I came up with me mouth full, he'd disappeared among the bodies. He always cheated but I knew I'd won.

I found some space and swam a few strokes. I were best at backstroke but when it were crowded like that you bumped into people all the time or hit them in the face when your hands come over yer 'ead. So I did breaststroke. You can see where you're going wi' breaststroke. But someone got in me way and I had to stop. It were the mermaid. She smiled. It were a real nice smile. She wore one a them rubber caps. White. Her bathers were white too and had little bubble things everywhere. It was the way they were stitched, I think, that did it. The costume showed 'er arms and 'er shoulders. They were pink where she'd been in the sun. Then she were gone. I saw her again on the other side of the crowded pool. She were looking at me. I got a funny feeling in me belly, like being on the front seat of a double decker trolley bus when it was going headlong down Church Bank, frightening and exciting at the same time.

I tried to swim towards her doing the Australian crawl because it made ya look good when you could really do it. I couldn't. But I'd have looked stupid doing backstroke.

Michael appeared next to me. 'Ah can swim all the way across underwater. Bet you can't,' he boasted.

'Ah can do the length,' I told him, and kept going. I tried once. I thought I were gonna drown. One of the big kids in school could do it. I'd seen him. I'd have needed to practise when there was more room.

Mermaid disappeared. Then she bobbed up again and was looking at me. She didn't smile or anything, just looked. She didn't seem to be with anyone.

By the time I got to her, she'd gone. I mean, where she was, she wasn't. Maybe she hadn't been looking at me at all. Maybe she'd been looking at someone behind me.

I didn't know what had happened to Michael. He were always bragging about what he could do; most of the time he couldn't. The attendant might have chucked him out for messing about.

Suddenly the mermaid was next to me again. 'Ah saw ya looking,' she said.

'Ah wasn't.' I knew ya should never let girls know that you're looking at 'em. 'I'm trying to find Michael. He's me brother.'

She stood in front of me, water up to her waist. Her cozzie was too big. It hung loose and I could see her titties under her togs, like two little raspberries. I tried not to look – but I tried to look as well.

'He might have drowned,' she said. She didn't smile at her joke. I thought it were a joke.

'No, no, he's a good swimmer.'

'You are too. I saw ya.'

I wondered which stroke I were doing. That were the trouble when it were crowded, you couldn't show how good you were.

'So are you. You stayed under for ages,' I told her.

She nodded, as though it was good to be told something nice.

I was close enough to touch her. But I daren't. I were close enough to kiss her.

Michael surfaced next to me. He didn't even notice I was talking to her. He were just so ignorant sometimes.

'I did a whole length underwater,' he bragged, blowing a stream of water in me face.

'Gi' over, will ya!' I told him.

He were always lying. There wasn't enough room to swim a length on top let alone under water.

Michael realised I wasn't interested in him. Then he saw the mermaid standing in front me. He looked at her and looked at me. 'Come on, let's do something,' he said.

I ignored him. I couldn't tek my eyes off her.

'Come on,' Michael said.

'Later.'

Michael still thought girls were stupid.

'What's yer name?' I asked the mermaid.

'Kathleen.'

I told her I liked it. I've got a cousin with the same name. Then I told her mine, Danny.

'I like yours too.'

I couldn't think of anything else to say.

'Danny! Come on.' Michael tugged me arm.

I ignored him. I wished he'd bugger off.

He swam away without looking back.

I still couldn't think of anything to say to Kathleen. What did other people talk about?

She stretched out a hand to me.

I took hold. It were cold and warm at the same time. She drew me along the pool out of the shallow end towards the deep end where you couldn't even see the bottom.

We began to swim side by side. I did breaststroke. So did she. She kept looking at me but never smiled except with her eyes. We reached the end of the pool, stopped and hung on to the side, close together. I could touch her sunburned shoulders. She hitched up the straps of her loose togs, hiding her titties. I tried not to look. I wondered if she knew I could see 'em.

'It's crowded, init?' I said.

She nodded. 'That's 'cause it's hot.'

It were my turn to nod.

Why couldn't I think of something clever to say? I coulda said something about famous swimmers from our town, but there weren't any.

'Michael's me brother,' I told her.

She smiled.

Michael would like to be a famous boxer but he won't be. He's too soft.

'Where's your mates?' I asked.

'Ah'm by miself.'

'Do ya want to race to the other end?' I asked. Then I thought, what if she beats me? What if she's a better swimmer than me?

She shook her head. 'No room.' She turned away, then looked and smiled wi' the tight lips she had.

'Where'd ya live?' I asked.

'Not far. You?'

'East Moor.'

'It's nice there.'

Her voice were soft, almost a whisper. Maybe she'd swallowed a lot of water. I had. Chlorine gets to some people.

'It's all right. We came into the centre on the trolleybus and walked up.'

Then we were quiet. Both of us looked around like we were trying to find someone, which we weren't.

Kathleen let go of the side of the pool and trod water. I trod water too and we bobbed up and down facing each other. It didn't seem to matter about talking any more.

I touched her arm, just brushed it. She looked at me but didn't say anything.

She felt for me hand, found it and held it tight, underwater where no one could see. It were like going downhill again on the top deck of the trolleybus, only the hill was steeper an' the bus faster. She came real close and our legs touched. We stayed like that.

Then she let go. 'I've gotta be off.'

'Not yet.'

She slowly moved away.

'Stay a bit longer,' I pleaded.

'I have ta go. I'll see ya outside.' She swam to the edge of the pool and got out, her too-big costume dripping water.

I didn't wait for Michael. I collected me clothes and get dressed so fast.

I stood by the entrance but she didn't come out. She'd decided not to bother wi' me and gone straight home. I wished that I'd waited for Michael, but they wouldn't let me back in to find him.

Other kids stepped out into the burning sun.

Then she appeared. She were nothing like a mermaid now. She walked over, a thin, grey towel rolled up under her arm. She were smaller than in the pool. Her hair, long, still wet, hung down to her shoulders in strings, dripping water onto a baggy dress that was once coloured but were now no colour. The dress had puffy little sleeves but one hung loose where something were broken. On her feet she had pumps that were worn through at the toes. One of them had no laces.

She smiled at me. This time her mouth was open. She had holes in her teeth. That's why she kept her mouth shut.

I smiled back. I had some fillings but ya couldn't see 'em unless ya looked real close.

'It were nice, weren't it? In the pool,' she said.

I nodded.

I wished I could have thought of something.

I wished I'd waited for Michael.

I wished I was anywhere but there.

'You comin' agin tomorrer?' she asked.

'I, I, ah don't know.'

'D'ya wanta walk part the way 'ome wi' me? It's not far.'

'Where?'

She hesitated. 'White Abbey.'

'Me Mam said I have to be home early. I've, I've, I've just remembered.'

I looked around for Michael. He came out.

'I've got ta go. Me an' Michael, have ta go.'

I grabbed Michael by the arm and took off before he could say what's up?

I turned as we ran down the hill. Kathleen was walking slowly in the direction of home, 'Shite Abbey'.

Interstate

I didn't know Nick very well, just enough to share a beer and a yarn. He was always on the quiet side and that night when I went into the Wallace he was tucked into a corner by himself.

I went over and said 'G'day.'

He looked up and nodded.

Balmain at that time was a working suburb, not a trendy suburb, definitely not trendy. There was a container terminal and small ship repair yards all the way along the peninsular. Two big factories, Colgate Palmolive and Unilever, contributed their particularly sweet stink to the suburb on hot summer days.

There were more pubs than any suburb in Australia, and no shortage of people to drink in them. No fancy restaurants, though, just one Chinese, one Greek.

I got a schooner and pulled up a stool next to Nick. He barely looked up. He kept staring out the open window, as though watching the line of smoke from his cigarette as it crept into the hot evening.

He was still in his work gear. His once-white overalls were layered with paint and muck which had become part of the fabric. His hands were stained and cracked. He was a P & D, a member of the Painters and Dockers union, which had its offices up the street from the pub. Ps & Ds did the crappiest jobs in the shipyards; cleaning the inside of tanks, scraping off the rust, the flaking paint and barnacles from the sides of ships when they were in the dry dock. I'm a welder, that's white-collar in comparison.

We both worked in the big government shipyard at Cockatoo Island, half a kilometre out in the Parramatta River. That's how we knew each other. The island's been closed for years now, ever since the government moved the work offshore where labour's cheaper. We occupied the island for weeks trying to save the jobs but it had no effect.

I lit a smoke and had a sip of cold beer. It was coming up Christmas and I couldn't wait to get away for a couple of weeks up the coast.

'How's it going?' I asked Nick.

He looked up from the open window. 'Oh, all right, I guess.' He had black bags under his eyes, like he hadn't slept for a week. Then he turned away again.

Like I said, Nick was never a talk talk sort of bloke, but this was quiet even for him.

So I let him be, and turned to watch a couple of guys and two girls playing pool. I'd noticed one of the guys before, sitting by himself across from Nick and me, staring. He was a big bloke with long black hair and wore a T-shirt with something written on it that I couldn't work out from where I sat.

The girls were better players than the guys. An' good-looking too – the girls, I mean, in case you get the wrong idea. The blonde was a real cracker.

After a while, I tried again with Nick. 'Anything planned for Christmas?'

He took a swig of his beer, then another. 'Yeah. Interstate. Probably.'

'Sounds good. Where?'

'Melbourne.'

'Ah, maybe not so good then,' I joked.

'You might be right at that.' He skolled his beer and got up from his stool. 'Another?' he asked me.

'Why not?'

He went off to the bar and I downed the rest of my drink.

I noticed another bloke from the Island say g'day to Nick, but Nick didn't seem to see him, just leaned on the bar, looking at nothing as he waited for the beers.

He brought them over and set them down on the table. He had a sip and went back to looking out the window. But he wasn't so much looking into the street, as looking way beyond, at something I couldn't see.

I wasn't going to get much conversation from him, so I turned to watch the pool players again but they were gone, gone from the pool table anyway. The blonde was now with the T-shirt guy. Most of the Ps & Ds in Sydney were Italians from Leichhardt, the next suburb. This guy looked more Irish.

I hadn't noticed before, but the blonde was very big in the hips. Funny how you don't see things the first time, or you notice some things but not others. The T-shirt guy glared at me. Probably the jealous type, the sort who would come up to you and say, 'Who the fuck youse looking at?' then belt you. I turned away.

The Friday evening regulars were drifting in and settling down in their favourite spots. One or two of the guys nodded in my direction the way blokes do in a pub and I nodded back.

'Ya got family in Melbourne?' I asked Nick.

He shook his head.

'Mates?'

'Aha, one or two, sort of.'

It was like getting blood from a stone.

He took a few more swigs of beer, then he started to open up. 'I'm gonna be working.'

'At Christmas? What, a department store Santa?'

He shook his head without cracking a smile. 'Nah. For the Melbourne lot, the Ps & Ds.'

'I'm not with ya,' I said. 'Why go all the way down there?'

'Not to scrape shit off the side of a boat,' he said, and downed his beer in one. He got up and went off to the loo.

As I waited for him to come back, I thought about the Melbourne branch of the Ps & Ds. It'd been being taken over by Irish crims. Micks. Real heavy stuff. Maybe what they'd learned in the IRA, or the UDA. There'd been a lot about it in the papers.

I half expected Nick not to come back, but he did, with two more beers. His hands trembled as he put them em the table.

'It was my shout,' I told him.

'Don't worry.'

I sucked in a mouthful, and waited.

He had a long drink, then tried to grin.

'You gonna tell me more?' I asked.

'It's the sort of job I've never done before. The money's real good. I need it'

'So what's the problem?'

'I don't want to. But there's no way I can get out of it.

'I still don't get it, the money's good, you don't want to do it, but you can't get out of it, right?'

'Yeah.'

I waited.

'It's the gun. A shotgun. I've never done that before.'

I wasn't sure I'd understood. My first thought for some reason was, rabbits, he's talking about shooting rabbits. Then I had another thought. Shit.

'Kill someone?' I asked, expecting him to say, 'Don't be bloody stupid.'

He didn't reply for a minute then he said, 'I shouldn't be telling ya.'

Too bloody right he shouldn't. I couldn't believe what he'd said. He didn't seem that sort of bloke in a million years.

'Not a good idea, Nick. Don't do it.'

Nick picked up his beer, then set it down again without drinking. 'I've gotta,' his lips clamped together in a tight, thin line. He suddenly stood. 'Have a good Christmas,' then he was gone before I could say anything else.

I left a couple of minutes later. Nick was just down the hill from the pub. His arms were stretched out above his head, propping against the wall, his legs spread wide. I thought he was spewing. He turned when I approached. His face was a mass of blood.

'S'all right,' he mumbled.

'Bullshit's all right.'

'I said s'all right,' he snarled.

'I'll take ya to hospital.'

'No ya won't.' He straightened and wiped his face with a sleeve.

'Something might be broken.'

'Mind your own business.'

'I just…'

'Keep your nose out! OK?'

'Who done it?'

'I fell.'

'I'll give ya a lift home.'

Nick shook his head. 'Go away.'

He steadied himself against the wall. 'I've gotta train ta catch tomorrow.'

He shuffled off. I watched him wobble down the hill, stumbling every few metres. I followed for a while, but there's nothing ya can do if someone doesn't want help.

Somebody had something on him. Forcing him to do it. That's for sure. He wasn't the kinda bloke to kill.

*

Maybe I shoulda told the cops. But I never.

A coupla days later, I went up the central coast fishing with some mates from Cockatoo. I didn't mention Nick or his bashing.

I kept my eyes on the news. One day there was a story about a P & D official in Melbourne who'd been blasted with a shotgun. He survived. But it was touch and go for a while.

Nick never came back to Cockatoo.

Lucky

Scratch is not the most beautiful chicken in the coop; feathers that should be long are short, and feathers that should be short are long. Some feathers grow entirely in the wrong direction.

Each night, Scratch flutters up to the highest perch in the coop away from everyone. When daylight comes, she jumps down from the perch to scratch in the dirt, like an upside-down, inside-out feather duster.

Scratch is not only back-to-front and inside-out, she's little. Because she's little, she gets pushed aside. Because she gets pushed aside, she doesn't get enough food and she doesn't grow much.

But Scratch doesn't care what she looks like, or if she does care it doesn't show The other chickens in the coop are her mother Henny; her sisters Peck, Flyby, Noisy, Cluck-Cluck and Cheep-Cheep; and her dad, Caesar, with his big, golden crown.

Scratch, and all the other chooks, are guarded by Little Jack when they come out of the coop. He watches over them with a big stick in his hand, cut for him by his nan. Scratch is Little Jack's favourite because he too is, like his name, little.

Every morning he and Nan come down from the house bringing the sun and chicken food. When all the chooks are squabbling and gobbling, Nan and Little Jack take the eggs from their nesting boxes; one box is a big old computer without its insides, two are old microwave ovens, the fourth is the styrofoam box that Nan's new computer came in.

Nan thinks the relationship is a fair one. She and Little Jack provide a free home, free food, free range, free protection – in return they and their friends get free eggs.

The other chooks bump Scratch out of the way as they scurry around, peck, peck, pecking, chork, chork, chorking.

When the chooks have been fed, Little Jack and his Nan look up at the blue sky. Is there a wedge-tailed eagle up there waiting to swoop?

Then they look across the tussocky paddock to the belt of gum trees swaying in the breeze. There might be a fox, nose twitching, sniffing the wind, watching. Waiting.

This morning, all is clear. Nan opens the rickety door to the coop. Little Jack stands aside, stick in hand, as the chooks pour out: Caesar first, then Henny; then Peck, Flyby, Noisy, Cluck-Cluck and Cheep-Cheep; and finally Scratch. They cluck and chuck and dig and delve.

Scratch wanders off into the grass away from Henny, away from her sisters. She is thinking only of what she can eat: seeds; leaping grasshoppers; snails; maybe a worm or two. The sun is warm, the sky is blue. She wanders further, and further, ever closer to the trees were she knowns there is a nest of juicy ants.

Little Jack calls out, 'Scratch! Come back here!'

Scratch ignores him. She is thinking about ants.

Little Jack calls out again, 'Scratch! Come back here!'

Scratch keeps on walking and pecking, heading for the trees. She doesn't see Fox, crouching behind a tree stump.

Fox springs.

He misses.

Scratch screeches in alarm, turns tail and scurries as fast as she can toward Jack and the coop. The rest of the family explodes in panic.

Caesar screams, 'Run run run run everybody run!'

Little Jack waves his stick in the air and charges Fox, screaming, 'Get away! Leave Scratch alone!'

Fox leaps again. This time he doesn't miss.

Little Jack swings his stick at the red bushy tail as it disappears among the trees.

The only sign of Scratch is a tiny pile of feathers drifting in the breeze.

Little Jack stands, looking, the stick hanging by his side. Tears trickle down his face.

Fox is gone. Scratch is firmly in his mouth, hurtling along just above the ground, faster than she has ever moved in her life. The world flashes by: grass; trees; rocks; a dirt road; cows; horses.

Eventually, Fox stops. He sits and looks down his long, thin nose at Scratch, held firmly in his jaws. Scratch looks back with tiny black, frightened eyes.

Fox throws back his head and tries to swallow. Scratch kicks and struggles. Fox tries again but he can't get Scratch down – the feathers are pointing the wrong way; they stick in his throat and tickle his tongue.

Scratch lies limp. Her feathers are sticky with Fox saliva. But her little black eyes are still open, staring Fox in the face.

Fox jiggles Scratch around in his mouth and tries again. Scratch will not go down his gullet. He has never had such a difficult dinner. Fox drops Scratch onto the ground so he can get a better grip.

Instantly the little hen is up and running. Running running rrrrunning!

Fox springs after the dinner that's disappearing in the direction of an ancient pine tree.

Scratch's little legs are going so fast that they're invisible. It's a run for life. A chicken run. Leaves and twigs fly in the air. Scratch is almost at the tree. Fox is chasing dinner and he almost has it.

Scratch hears the click of teeth behind her. She launches herself at the lowest branch and scurries up. Fox stops. He lifts his chin and looks up into the tree. Scratch is shaking like a wet feather duster. Fox licks his lips and steps delicately onto a low-hanging branch. He begins to climb.

Scratch flaps and scrambles ahead of him. Fox advances. Scratch clucks in terror. She climbs higher. Fox follows. Scratch struggles higher still. Fox is behind, drooling with thoughts of dinner.

Scratch keeps going. Fox follows, but the branch bends and sways.

Fox almost loses his balance. He is too heavy to go further. He retreats. He sits at the foot of the tree and looks up at Scratch almost out of sight.

Fox curls into a ball, his long bushy red tail wraps around him. Only his nose and eyes are free. He waits.

The sun goes down. Darkness comes.

All night long, Scratch clings to her perch. She is lonely and misses her mother Henny; her sisters Peck, Flyby, Noisy, Cluck-Cluck and Cheep-Chee; her dad Caesar; and Little Jack. She fluffs out her wet feathers and tries to keep warm.

When the morning sun touches the top of the tree with gold, she awakens and looks to the ground far below. There is no sign of Fox.

Slowly, Scratch descends, fluttering down, branch to branch. Her little eyes check the ground. Is Fox hiding behind a grass tussock? Is he concealed by a tree? Where is he waiting to pounce?

Scratch is hungry. Below, ants are scurrying about in the sun. Scratch flutters down branch to branch. She lands on the ground, and waits, ready to flap back into the tree.

Nothing happens. Fox is gone.

Scratch starts to eat. When she has had her fill, she points her beak in the direction of home.

She limps past the horses in the paddock. She looks up at the sky for the wedge-tailed eagle, and down on the ground for Fox. When the sun sets, Scratch wearily scrambles up a tree to the topmost branches, fluffs up her feathers and sleeps – with one eye open. A silver moon shines on her. Next morning the sun rises, warm and red.

Scratch sets off again, even though her toes are cut and sore and she can hardly walk. She passes the cows. She re-crosses the road.

The first one to see Scratch coming through the tufty grass is Caesar. He throws back his head and cock-a-doodle-doodles louder than he has ever cock-a-doodle-doodled before. The rest of the family run towards him in panic.

Little Jack looks at Caesar. Why is he making all that noise? He takes a tighter grip on his stick and steps forwards. Is it Fox?

Then he sees Scratch. Scratch sticks out her chest and struts towards him. She doesn't care that most of her feathers are missing, that her tail is gone, and that her toes are almost too sore to step on. She has outwitted Fox, she is home.

Little Jack drops his stick, rushes forwards and scoops the scruffy chook into his arms. 'Scratch! Lovely Scratch.' He cuddles the nearly bald bird to his chest.

The rest of the family step aside as he carries Scratch into the coop. Nan brings extra food and they all gather round to share the feast.

'What a lucky chook you are,' Little Jack says, smiling.

That night, he lifts Scratch onto her perch. She looks down on the rest of the family with their beaks upturned admiringly. Caesar stands beneath. He throws back his head, shakes his golden crown and crows with delight. Scratch shuffles what is left of her feathers, and goes to sleep.

Nan changes Scratch's name. She now calls her Lucky.

But Little Jack knows Scratch didn't escape because she was lucky, she escaped because she didn't give in. No matter how small you are, if you don't give in, you can be smarter than Fox.

Beloved Man

I don't know why I got the emails. They were there when I did my morning login at 7.15. I don't usually get emails from women, or anyone else for that matter. I wondered how they got my email address. And why me?

The first one said,

Hi, My heart is open and kind for my beloved man. My dream in life is to meet the right husband for me. I am very appealing and positive lady, I love life, music, good weather and close people around me. Moreover I am family-orientated and I prefer a relationship based on mutual respect, love and understanding. I hope right now you are reading these lines, so write to me! I will wait That you smiled at me. I am live in Moscow.

Regards,

Ekaterina.

There was a photo. She was blonde. Early twenties. Quite pretty. A bit fleshy. Very Russian looking. I didn't reply. I didn't decide not to. I just didn't get around to it. At the time I wasn't looking for anyone.

The second email came from another woman a month later when I was still considering the first. It said,

Hi my friend, I only wish to write to you and tell my letter got to you. First I would like to speak a little about myself my name is Anna, 25 years. I live in Russia to Kirov. [I Looked up Kirov in Wikipedia and it said it is in Kyrgyzstan. It was once part of the Soviet Union I guess. But that was years ago. I don't know why she would say it's in Russia.] I was in agency and advised yours email that I could have acquaintance to you. And I only wanted that you have spent about 10 minutes looking, then received from you the answer you like to have acquaintance to me? I started to search for the man as me very alone and 28 years old. Moreover if you wish to being with correspondence or to begin acquaintance tell me your answer. I shall wait much. I hope that I can become your friend.

Can send me photo and story life on my email: annaplotjikk!@gmail.com

Anna!

Her photo showed a thin-faced woman looking nervously at the camera but smiling. She had dark reddish hair. Mum would have said, 'She dyes it. You can tell just by looking.'

Every woman dyes her hair these days.

The only recent photo of me was taken with Mum just after she had been admitted to Flower Bank nursing home. It was in the little garden, near the rose bushes. She always loved roses. We both wrote our names on the photo and I framed it. She stood it on the little cabinet next to her bed where she kept her hairbrush. I used to brush her hair every day and she'd tell me, 'You're a good son. You've always put me first.'

Then one day she didn't remember who I was. It happened quickly. I couldn't believe it. She'd said, 'Who are you? I know your face, I think, but I can't put a name to it.'

I still went to see her every day and weekends but didn't stay so long. That's when I started logging in on the internet before I went to work. I'd have breakfast, then log in at 7.15. I felt it was important to have a routine. I'd Google wherever my fancy took me. Sometimes I'd click on country towns and look at the photos. From there I'd just follow links. It's amazing where you end up. Norway was a favourite. I'd like to go one day. But it's a long way. I limited myself to half-an-hour a day. I made a list of places I might visit.

I don't know what happened to the photo of Mum and me. When I picked up Mum's belongings after she died, it was gone. Jessica, the Filipina woman in charge, said she would try to find it. I rang her a few times, then I gave up. Jessica was a nice woman. Kind. I really liked her. But she left and I never saw her again. The Philippines would be interesting too.

I put Mum's things in her bedroom. Her clothes hung in the wardrobe and the hairbrush was on her dressing table. Pity I didn't have the signed photo in the frame.

Eventually I decided to reply to both Ekaterina and Anna to see what would happen. You need something to get you out of bed in the morning people always say. The internet isn't enough.

I'd actually tried an Australian dating site in the past, when Mum was first put into Flower Bank and I was alone and I had some free time, the first for years. I'd put in my details and uploaded the photo of me next to the rose trees, with Mum cropped out. I didn't look too bad. I was smiling so it didn't show my thick lips too much. And I had a haircut, short, so it didn't show that my hair was thinning. With the photo you include information about yourself, what you like and dislike. I couldn't think of things that interested me, so I checked out other profiles.

I just said I liked going for walks, which I do; watching TV; going to the movies, which I hadn't done much because that would have meant leaving Mum alone; watching stupid YouTube videos, they're hilarious. Then I made a few things up, like hanging out with friends; going to the gym; swimming; and listening to music. But I dropped them all except music, because if I met someone, they would know that I didn't like doing any of those others. But everyone likes music, more or less.

I was surprised at the dating site. I thought the women wouldn't be attractive. But they were. Most of them were really pretty. I knew they would put up their best photos but you can't make yourself beautiful if you're ugly – and the site guaranteed that the photos were genuine. Sometimes they only showed a head and face. They could have had the body of a dog, or a horse – a centaur. It made me wonder why. What was wrong with their body? Maybe they were really fat, really thin, or shaped like a pear, or something. One or two looked like sex workers. But you can't judge a book by its cover. They almost all looked super confident. Most said they had been to college. I'm not sure what that means, whether it's uni or just a local TAFE.

The profiles are made up by ticking boxes and don't tell you much. One woman said she had cancer. Why would you admit that when you were looking for a partner? Then I realised she said she was born under Cancer, the Zodiac sign. They all said which sign they were born under: Gemini, Virgo, Leo, or whatever. What relevance did that ever have? It told you nothing about a person. It must be one of the boxes they are asked to tick. Most claimed to be Christians. Most said they didn't smoke. I don't either. It's a disgusting habit. I couldn't image kissing someone who smoked. I didn't follow up on those who posed with a glass of wine in their hand or showed their boobs too much. Boobs are OK, but not when they are stuck in your face in a photo. I don't drink, so there was no point in dating a party girl.

Some were separated or divorced. I didn't want to go there either. You keep hearing of demented, jealous exes who murder their former partners and their lovers. I read of one guy who chopped up his ex and her new husband and put them in garbage bags – her head with the guy's body, and the guy's head with her body. How bad is that?

A number of women had kids. I crossed them off right away. I've got nothing against kids, but I don't want to be a babysitter for some guy who has abandoned his responsibilities.

The Australian women wanted the same thing as the Russian women: respect, a genuine and honest guy not into playing games, or, as one put it dead straight: 'If you're here for sex, or hook-ups, sorry, not interested, you can go to the next girl.' All right by me.

They were all so attractive, even the one who gave her height at four feet. I thought that was probably a mistake, then I came across another who said she was four feet four inches, quite a bit taller. I suppose there are men out there too who are vertically challenged, or whatever the description is. I couldn't understand why the normal ones didn't have a regular partner. I suppose they just didn't meet anyone they liked among their friends, or in a pub or club or wherever people hook-up.

There was one I particularly fancied who happened to live in Bankstown, the same suburb as me. She was called Miranda. That's the name of a suburb too, not far away. A coincidence. Or an omen. She had a very sweet face. She was slender, not one of those busty types. She described her body as athletic. Another ticked box probably. I couldn't imagine her playing rugby or soccer. I'm not into sport either.

She said she liked ambition and intellect in a guy; someone independent, who can converse, make a girl laugh, yet respect autonomy. If the man can cook, it's a bonus but not essential, she said.

I can cook a bit now that Mum's passed on. Mainly chops. But I'm not sure about the other things. Conversing? Making a girl laugh? How do you make someone laugh? Tickling might work. I know some girls at work laugh at me behind my back. Mum always said I'd get along better with people if I had a sense of humour. She was one to talk. She was kind, but not big on laughing. I probably get it from her.

I don't know what respecting autonomy means either. Whatever you want I suppose. It could mean one of those open-ended marriages. I don't fancy that.

'You didn't come home last night, darling?'

'No. I slept with someone I met at the pub.'

'No worries, darling.'

I don't think so. But it could just mean leaving someone alone with their thoughts when they wanted it. I'd be OK with that. I like to be left with my thoughts. Most of the time, in fact.

I knew it was a long shot, but I decided to look for Miranda in the street and see if she really was like her photo. If she did, I could message her. I walked up and down Bankstown's main drag at different times and sat in the coffee shops. No one looked like her. Maybe she didn't go out much. Or maybe her photo wasn't a good likeness. It was a stupid idea anyway.

Eventually I sent her a message. She was no longer available. I'd left it too late. Mum always said, 'Thomas, you're as slow as a wet weekend.'

I was disappointed about Miranda. I wonder what the guy was like.

Once I had registered and put my picture up, a lot of women viewed me and wanted to make contact. I've never thought I was particularly bad-looking, but I was surprised at the response. None of them appealed to me, though. They were almost all beautiful. And confident-looking. Enough to scare you. Seeing them up there made me feel sad. Were they desperate to find someone to love? Or is that just the way things are done these days? It gives you a chance to find out something about them before you go on a date.

I think it's normal now. I mean, that's what I was doing.

After Miranda, I tried a few others. But there were so many. Cyberspace is full of women looking for men and, I suppose, men looking for women. Otherwise it wouldn't work. They are all floating around out there looking through telescopes. Every day I got a message, '30 new singles we think you'd like', or similar. Sometimes an individual would want me to contact them. Or I'd just click on one of the names I fancied, like Welshie for instance. I liked that name. But she was mad as a cut snake. You could tell by her eyes. And all her photos were with guys wearing bandanas round their heads like they wanted to be Rambo. Why would you put up photos of yourself with guys if you were looking for a partner?

All that was in the past. There was nothing I could have done anyway because Mum was still. alive. It was wishful thinking. But the new Russian emails got me wondering again. There was something about them that appealed. I checked out a website called Russian Brides. It said that over-independence and feminism haven't spoiled Russian women's belief in traditional family values. Although I didn't think that the women on the site particularly looked the family type.

The site also said that Russian women were not concerned about age differences the way women are in the West, and ten, or fifteen years, or more, don't matter. So I could attract a woman who was in her twenties, like Ekaterina. I decided to see if she was still looking for a man. I emailed her my photo and told her a few things about myself, the same as on the Australian site: what I liked (I dropped the reference to watching stupid YouTube videos); that I'd worked in the office of the state electricity network since I left school over twenty years ago; that Mum had died and that I lived in the house by myself and I was lonely.

I looked up the meaning of Ekaterina – 'pure'.

There was no reply. I was about to try Anna when Ekaterina got back to me.

> My beloved man I had stopped hope that you would not speak with me. Now I am so happy. Your photo is a handsome man. I sad your mother and that you are lonely and alone in your home. I too am lonely. My mother she died and no father. I would make each other happy. Yes?

She must have been waiting all that time for me to respond – or other guys hadn't come up to her expectations.

She said she was a teacher. She went on to tell me the things she liked. They were the same as me: watching TV; going for walks; movies. A good start. She asked me what music I preferred. That put me in a bit of a spot. I like music in general but it has never really grabbed me. Mum was the same. She just had the radio on, and whatever was being played she would half listen. She didn't like rock or anything loud, though. She said it made her head ache. So I'd choose a station for her, Classic FM, easy listening stuff, or something similar. Mum didn't like the commercial stations.

I emailed Ekaterina straight back. Because she was Russian, I said Tchaikovsky.

She immediately replied and said, 'Me too.'

I'd guessed right. Great.

So, we began emailing each other every day and she'd tell me things she did: walks along the banks of the Moskva River, that's what she called it; visiting the Kremlin and Saint Basil's Cathedral. I Googled them. Wow. We have nothing like that in Australia. She'd been to the Bolshoi Ballet. She was a really interesting woman. But without that overconfident thing Australian women have. She visited the Tretyakov Gallery. I Googled it too. The place has paintings going back a thousand years.

She kept saying how lonely it was doing these things by herself.

I needed to get out of the house more so I had things to write about. I couldn't just keep telling her about what I'd seen on TV.

I had never been to an art gallery. So I went. The Art Gallery of NSW. It was great. I told Ekaterina that I liked Brett Whitely's stuff. He's Australian, sort of modern. I thought liking him would make me seem up to date and younger. I went to the Australian Museum too. I hadn't been since I was dragged along on a school excursion. It was different. People didn't creep round in silence. And it was full of kids, talking and laughing and holding hands. I was there the whole day. I regret not taking Mum when she was alive.

I told Ekaterina. She said she'd love to see them with me, and the Opera House, and the Harbour, and Bondi Beach. She also said she wanted to go to college so she could get on in Australia. She told me how respectful and smart and gentle I must be. Which was nice. No one has said that before. Certainly not Mum.

Well, to cut a long story short, she said that she was sure I was the man she had been looking for. But her heart was breaking because she did not have enough money to come to Australia to meet me yet.

I wondered whether I should go to Moscow, then if it worked, bring her back to Australia. We had a lot in common and, although she was young, if you're Russian it doesn't matter. And she was pretty, but without that Australian cockiness.

It would cost a lot to fly to Russia and stay in Moscow. I didn't fancy the idea of flying anyway, so I decided to pay for her ticket to Australia. I don't have stacks of money but I've got a job, money in the bank, the house.

She was over the moon and kept telling me I was her beloved man and she was sure we would be very happy. I didn't tell anyone at work. We kept on emailing each other. She was still taking long walks around Moscow and going to galleries and telling me how much she wanted me to show her Sydney. Walking a long time makes my feet ache. She kept saying how she loved kids. I'm not so sure about that.

She asked me to describe Bondi Beach. I hadn't been since I was a kid. So I drove in from Bankstown at the weekend. I've never seen so many beautiful women – hardly any clothes on, and sticking out their breasts and backsides. The men had muscles on their muscles. I had a swim between the flags but the water was really rough.

It seemed to take forever for her visa to go through. But that's the Department of Immigration and Border Protection for you. And to be fair, they have to screen for possible terrorists. Some terrorists are Chechens, and Chechens live in Russia. You can't be too careful.

Eventually it happened. The visa was granted. I booked and paid for her flight and a week later I was standing at the arrivals gate in Sydney airport with my heart in my mouth and a piece of card in my hand. The card had one word written on it: 'Ekaterina'. I had thought of drawing a cupid with a bow or something but that would have been over the top. Besides, I can only draw matchstick people.

I felt stupid standing there holding up her name. All round me people were squealing and waving as arrivals emerged from the customs hall. Every time a woman came out, my stomach went into a knot. I wasn't sure I'd recognise her. I'd emailed her another photo of me that I'd found. Full length, so she would know that I had legs and arms and wasn't four feet tall. It didn't matter that it was a few years old.

People trickled out slowly. It seemed to go on forever. Finally there was just me, holding a card. Everyone else had gone.

I had a horrible sinking feeling. Like dropping in one of those really fast elevators.

What had I done? Had she arrived on my ticket then simply gone off?

I got a coffee and went back and stood there again just in case, cardboard message in one hand, cardboard coffee cup in the other. Maybe she'd had problems because she was Russian. They all used to be communists.

So I waited. I drained my coffee. I stood for a while with the empty cup in my hand.

I turned to leave and bumped into a woman.

'Sorry.'

The woman stood and looked at me. 'Thomas?' She pointed at my sign, then herself, 'Ekaterina'. She smiled.

Somehow we'd missed each other.

I jiggled the card. Then I held out my hand and shook her hand. It was soft and warm. I said 'Dobrahye ootrah', which means 'Good morning.'

We'd done it. All the fear flowed out of my body.

Ekaterina seemed excited and nervous all at the same time. She was shorter than I expected and stood looking up at me. Her eyes were wide open. Blue.

I didn't know whether to hug her or not. She didn't step forward so I decided not. And I wasn't sure this Ekaterina was the Ekaterina. This Ekaterina was not as young as the one in the photo.

She had a bag slung over her shoulder. That's all she had. I reached out and she passed it to me. It was amazingly heavy.

'You're here,' I said.

She smiled and nodded.

My heart was bang, bang, banging. I still couldn't think of what to say. Finally I heard my voice, 'Let's go home, eh?'

'Home,' for both of us. It sounded strange.

It was a long walk to the car. I hoped the car didn't put her off. It was an old Toyota. Not one you'd jump in the air about. Talking to someone online is different to talking to them face-to-face. I kept smiling at her, though.

I told her the car park was the most expensive in Australia. Possibly the world, and that I never parked there. 'Is it dear in Moscow?' I asked.

She nodded. She stayed by my side like she was afraid of getting lost. Her eyes were wide and she was looking around at everything. It must be really weird landing in a strange country. The nearest I'd had to overseas was Tasmania with Mum. Not exactly long-haul, and everyone there speaks the same language as us. Even then I'd been airsick.

I tried to imagine being met by someone you didn't really know but were going to marry. I couldn't. Then I realised I was in the same boat. Except the boat was my country.

I tried again to make conversation. The best I could manage was, 'How is Moscow? Is the river frozen?'

She smiled and nodded. 'Yes.'

She had red finge nails. But these were nice, like flower petals. Her face was round, with full cheeks. I noticed a crescent-shaped scar across her nose which I hadn't seen in her photo. Maybe it was new. She might have fallen on one of her walks.

She'd added a few kilos, and a few years since her photo, but I could see now that it was definitely her. She looked good, really. I wondered how I looked to her. The two pictures I'd sent were taken a few years ago, so I couldn't complain. But I hadn't changed. Not much anyway. I'd always meant to exercise more and eat less. Now I had a reason, and I'd be taking her for long walks like she did all the time in Moscow.

The drive from the airport to Bankstown is all M5 East Motorway except for the last couple of kilometres. We crawled. As we waited to go into the tunnel I told her, 'This is one of the longest tunnels in Australia, 3.8 kilometres.'

She nodded and smiled.

I don't know why I went that way. I hate tunnels. They scare me. I think of the millions of tons of rock and soil above and of it falling on me. On everyone. Or it collapsing at the entrance and exit, and being trapped and suffocating to death. Slowly. But Ekaterina would have been tired after the flight and that was the quickest way to get home.

In the tunnel, huge trucks towered above us and the drivers in their hi-vis shirts looked down like they were gods and we were insects about to be crushed.

'The longest tunnel's in Brisbane,' I shouted above the noise.

The Hume Highway is almost as noisy but at least you can breathe there.

Mum said I was claustrophobic because I was accidentally locked in a wardrobe when I was a kid and was too frightened, or stupid, to yell for help.

I'm not sure Ekaterina understood what I was saying because she didn't respond much. Eventually she said, 'Where the Opera House? Your Harbour Bridge?'

I pointed back over my shoulder, in the opposite direction to where we were going, and said, 'That way.'

She looked disappointed.

Maybe I'd given her the impression that I lived on the edge of Sydney Harbour.

I said I'd take her to the Opera House and the Bridge and everywhere, but not just then. I wondered how they'd compare with the Kremlin and St Basil's Cathedral.

As I drove, I kept looking at her out of the corner of my eyes. She had lovely white teeth that showed a lot because her mouth didn't quite close. Her hair was fair, and longer on top than the sides. It suited her. She wore a red leather jacket that matched her red fingernails, even though it was a warm spring day.

She must have realised I was looking because she reached out and put her hand on mine for a moment and squeezed it. She smiled. My heart jumped. I felt like I'd run a marathon. Not that I ever have. People have heart attacks doing it.

'The longest road tunnel in the world's in Norway, Lærdal, 24.51 kilometres. A lot longer than this.' I told her.

It was a stupid thing to say. Obviously 24.51 kilometres is longer than 3.8 kilometres. She must have thought I was a dill.

A marathon's 42.19 kilometres, so the Norway tunnel's about half a marathon. You could die running that too.

'Thank you,' she said.

When we got home, I showed her around the house and the garden. She loved the pots of Mum's orchids that lined both sides of the footpath.

Then I put her bag in Mum's old room. I didn't want to rush things. I'd printed off the photo of Mum and me next to the rose bushes and put it in a frame on the bedside table. I thought Ekaterina might like to see what Mum looked like and how close we were.

I had moved the hairbrush that was on the bedside table to my room. It still smelled of Mum's hair. And I'd pushed Mum's clothes down one end of the wardrobe. I hoped that Ekaterina didn't mind the smell of mothballs.

She said she was very tired and could she rest. I showed her the shower and left her to it. When she went into Mum's room, I thought I could hear her talking in a low voice, as though she was on the phone. Then I decided she must have been telling someone in Russia that she had landed OK. It takes a brave woman to fly halfway around the world like that.

I made dinner for her, Russian fish soup. I got the recipe from the internet. It was easy: fish stock from the supermarket, some vegies and fish. I hoped she'd like it.

I found one of Mum's tablecloths that she'd kept tucked in a drawer for special occasions – not that there had ever been any – and I covered the Formica table and laid out mats, the ones with Australian flora, and cutlery. We could go out to a restaurant later in the week, Viet or Leb – she could choose.

I'd bought tea lights and I set them in saucers of water so they couldn't burn anything. Then I decided that was a bit over the top and I put them back in the cupboard.

But I changed my mind again and put them out. What's wrong with being romantic occasionally? Mum would have turned the lights on and said, 'That's all very well but you've got to be able to see what you're eating.'

I sat at the table waiting for Ekaterina to waken. I watched the flickering tea lights. Ekaterina didn't waken. I wasn't sure whether to knock on the door or not. I decided to let her rest. I ate some of the Russian fish soup, it wasn't bad, and put the rest back in the fridge for later. I blew out the tea lights and went to bed.

I didn't sleep well. I could smell the wax for ages. Once, I thought I heard Ekaterina talking.

Next morning, she was still sleeping and I went for a walk. I didn't bother to log onto the internet before I went out. When I got back, she was sitting at the table in her red leather jacket and tight jeans. She had her hands clamped between her knees.

She looked up at me and smiled. 'Sorry. Last night I sleeped.'

She looked gorgeous.

I just said, 'No worries. Do you want breakfast? Do you like eggs? Do you like muesli?'

She said yes and asked me if I had 'orypeu'. Her eyebrows went up in hopeful question mark.

'Or…?'

She mimed a shape with her hands. It looked a bit rude.

She took out her phone, dabbed it a few times with her finger, then looked at me with an expression of triumph. 'Cu-cum-ber.'

'Aaah! Sorry, no.'

I got everything ready and made toast while she watched. Then we ate.

She told me what had happened to her luggage. Someone had stolen it at Moscow airport and all she had was what she was wearing and a few things in her carry-on bag.

*

I took her to Target in Bankstown to get some clothes. It's as good as anywhere. But you don't pay through the nose. When we got inside, she walked around a bit with me in tow. She didn't seem to find anything she liked.

After a couple of minutes, I said, 'No?'

I could tell by the look on her face that she wasn't impressed. I shop for clothes once year, at Target. But I could see her point. Clothes are important to women. Men don't care. Mum always said, 'Clothes don't maketh the man, women maketh the man.'

I felt mean, so we jumped on the train into the city. Every suburban station we stopped at was like a new country because of the different nationalities. I'd heard Pitt Street Mall was pretty good for fancy stuff. It was. And it cost a bit. I paid for Ekaterina's new things before she could offer, then we sat down in one of those old arcades. I felt pretty good, coffee and cakes, Ekaterina looking very glam in her new clothes. More than one guy looked at her, then looked at me. I could tell they were jealous. We talked, as best we could, and made plans for the next few days.

I took her to Circular Quay and the Opera House. You don't take much notice of these things when you live here, and I've never gone into the city much. Because Ekaterina was into art, and I was learning, we went to the gallery. There are some huge old paintings, really famous Australian landscapes. They were done by people that I'd read about on the net: Botticelli, Leonardo da Vinci and Rubens. Ekaterina held my hand and that was really nice. I asked her if the NSW gallery was as good as the Tretyakov Gallery in Moscow but she didn't understand. I reminded her of her emails, then she remembered, and she said this was very good.

We went back home after that so she could sleep and she kissed me on the cheek before she went into Mum's room, her room now, and closed the door.

I thought our first day out together was a success. We hadn't talked much but that was understandable; she was still jet-lagged. That and the language difference. But she was smart and would improve quickly now she was living with me.

I got a surprise when we sat down for dinner. I'd cooked something traditionally Australian: roast lamb – the remains of the fish soup were in the freezer. She produced a bottle of vodka. I'd got the impression she was like me and didn't drink.

She persuaded me to try some and she made a toast, 'To us.'

I got the feeling she'd practised that to get it right. 'To us,' I replied and sipped the vodka.

'*Nyeht*,' she laughed and shook her head. 'This!' She downed her shot in one gulp.

I did the same to make her feel at home. Wow!

She said the dinner was '*Ochen horosho*,' then explained that meant, 'Very good.'

That was nice to know.

It hadn't occurred to me before, but I wondered if she could cook. The websites said that Russian women were much more family orientated than their Western counterparts. I assumed that meant things like cooking. I would find out. Not that it mattered.

Ekaterina proposed another toast, 'To Aus-tray-lia. To future.'

We skolled our vodka again.

Then another toast, my turn, 'To Russia.'

'To Russia.' Ekaterina started to sing softly. In Russian.

Her voice was sad. She was probably homesick. I've never been homesick, even when I went to Tasmania.

I'm not used to alcohol. I woke next morning in my bed. She was in hers. I had a hangover. What I remembered of the night before was fun.

When we were having breakfast, Ekaterina told me she felt we should wait till we were married before we slept together. She said she was traditional that way. She looked at me in a sort of defiant manner, waiting for my response, as though she was afraid of what I'd say. The scar on her nose seemed more prominent when she was tense.

I don't know what it had to do with Russian tradition. It's not what I expected. It is the twenty-first century. In the West, people seem to have sex before they know each other's names these days. Sometimes I think they do it before they even meet. But that didn't seem to have spread to Russia.

I didn't know what to say. It's not really the sort of thing you want to argue about with your bride-to-be. I respected her for it. And it meant that I was going to be the first. That wouldn't have been the case with an Australian woman of her age, that's for sure.

Ekaterina kept to what had been Mum's bedroom, and I kept to mine.

I noticed through the open door one day that she had taken the photo of Mum and me from the bedside table.

The fact that we had separate rooms didn't stop us enjoying time together. We took the ferry to Manly, and Ekaterina loved the way the harbour sparkled in the sun.

We swam at Bondi. She wasn't very good and the waves scared her. I put an arm around her as we came out of the water. Her skin was as pale as milk. She was cold and soft and covered in goosebumps and salt water droplets. I tried to lick them off. But she pushed me away and laughed, then ran up the beach to her towel.

*

We got married as soon as I could organise it. It was a very small thing, at the registry office. I had no family. She had no family. I bought Ekaterina a new dress and shoes and stuff for the occasion. She looked fantastic. A bunch of yellow roses in her hands. She has such a smile. Her nails were painted red like when she arrived.

To give it the feeling of an occasion, I invited a couple of mates from work, Alan, who had the work station next to me, and Mark, who was on the other side. Both were nice guys, even if they did tease me a bit. But I'd shown them that I could pull a beautiful chick. They brought their wives, Meredith and Sophie. Two blondes. Mum always said, 'Never trust a bottle blonde.' That would exclude half the female population of Sydney. Looking back, I realised that Mum must have had a thing about women's hair, possibly because hers always looked like it was a paddock in the middle of drought. I'd met Meredith and Sophie before at an office function. They were all right.

Alan and Mark were impressed with Ekaterina. Alan hugged her, a bit too much, and told her, 'When you've finished with this drop-kick, give me a ring.'

Meredith flashed him one of those looks that wives keep for their husbands when they're disgusted with them.

Mark said, 'No wonder he's been keeping you to himself. He told us you were ugly and we wouldn't want to meet you.'

I hadn't said anything like that.

Meredith and Sophie told her she was beautiful, and I was lucky. I agreed. I was lucky. I'm not sure how much Ekaterina understood.

We had lunch in a George Street pub after the ceremony, my shout. They toasted us in vodka. Meredith and Sophie got the giggles.

As wedding presents, Alan and Meredith bought us a copy of the *Kama Sutra*, and Mark and Sophie bought a super brightly glazed dip bowl (it said dip bowl on the box) shaped like a thong. I don't know whether Russians do that sort of joke stuff, or whether they buy people samovars, or big fur hats and things like that. Ekaterina blushed when she opened the *Kama Sutra*. It looked more like yoga exercises than sex to me. She didn't know what to make of the bowl. She looked at me with a funny expression as she held it out, then smiled at them and said, 'Spa-see-ba. Spa-see-ba.' She started to laugh.

They guests didn't stay long after that, which was a relief.

Ekaterina and me celebrated properly that evening with dinner at a smart restaurant at Circular Quay. I should have brought Mum here at least once in her life. But I hadn't. Too late for that sort of regret. I thought it worth lashing out a bit. After all, you don't get married very often. It was a warm evening and the lights sparkled on the Harbour.

The Bridge and the Opera House were lit up and people were walking slowly by and talking and taking selfies and enjoying life. There were locals and tourists from all over the world. It was a fairyland for grown-ups. We had a bottle of white wine with fish. I made sure that Ekaterina had the seat with the best view of the Harbour. She sat looking and didn't seem to be able to find words for it all. She held my hand under the table and I could smell the shampoo in her hair, or perfume.

I don't remember being so happy. Ever. I could have stayed there all night. But I wanted to get home so the two of us could be alone. Man and wife. Should we keep the *Kama Sutra*, or dump it and the thong bowl? As I sat admiring her admiring the view, I wondered how life was going to work out for us. I was sure it would be hard at times: two different cultures; her, thousands of kilometres from where she grew up. Neither of us had family, so we'd need each other.

Maybe Ekaterina read my thoughts, because she leaned across the table and kissed me gently on the mouth. My hair stood on end. I could feel it. I wondered if the people on the next table noticed. As she straightened, she knocked her wine glass onto the floor. The waiter came over, telling her not to worry. She didn't. Neither did I. We both laughed, and the waiter filled a new glass for her and called her 'Madam.'

After a while, I asked, 'Shall we go?'

'*Nyeht*,' she shook her head. Her blonde hair spun in the light. 'Stay more. It is so nice here. People, just being happy.'

I ordered another bottle of wine. Probably not a good idea. Now that I'd been introduced to vodka, I realised what I'd been missing. Or maybe it was just being with Ekaterina that made me realise what I'd been missing.

I was a bit wobbly when we left the restaurant…well, a lot wobbly, but Ekaterina seemed OK. We walked along the Quay and passed a fire-eating acrobat – maybe it was time for me to have a career change, maybe a tightrope walker, or a juggler.

I bought her a CD of Aboriginal didge music. Then I got two huge gelatos, hazelnut for her and caramel for me, because I know Russians love ice cream. You could hardly move for people and we wandered along slowly arm in arm.

The train to Bankstown was full of noisy young guys who'd had too much to drink.

I asked Ekaterina if it was like this in Moscow. 'Worse,' she said and pulled a face.

I dozed off at one stage and woke up with my head on her shoulder just before the train pulled into Bankstown. We walked home with Ekaterina propping me up.

Ekaterina ducked into the shower. I wanted to watch her but she closed the door, so I made a pot of tea while I waited. When I'd had my shower and put on my new dressing gown, she was gone. I thought she was waiting in my bedroom, our bedroom, but it was empty. I knocked on the door of her room. I tried the handle. It was locked.

I called out, 'Ekaterina! Open the door!'

'Please, Thomas, it is a long day.'

'We're married,' I said.

'I very tired. Let us please rest tonight.'

I pushed and pulled at the door but it didn't budge. I stood for ages, calling her name. But she didn't reply. I'd probably had too much to drink.

I sat on the couch and waited to see if she would come out. I must have fallen asleep because I woke up at first light busting to go to the loo and with a crick in my neck. As I passed Ekaterina's door, I could hear her talking. Maybe she was having a bad dream. But it didn't sound like dream talk.

When she got up, she didn't mention what had happened, except to say how wonderful dinner at the Quay had been and how kind I was.

I'd taken a week off work so we could get to know each other really close. I'd thought we could go into the city again and maybe visit the

Australian Museum and have a picnic across the road in Hyde Park. But I didn't feel like it after what had happened, or not happened.

Instead we made a start on the application for her partner visa which could take a year or more to go through. Once that was fixed, we'd apply for a permanent visa for her as my wife. It could then be another twenty-four months before that was OK.

I pulled two chairs up to the kitchen table and opened my laptop. We sat side by side. I could feel the warmth from her body and smell the shampoo in her hair. Our legs were touching. I liked that, being so close.

Only a government bureaucrat could think up something as complicated as what I opened online. Border Protection! I'm surprised even the rain can get in without being stopped and and wrung out. Maybe it can't and that's why we have so many droughts. We lined up the documents we needed. The list was endless – her passport, wedding certificate, we had to have proof we were cohabiting – did they want a selfie of us in bed together? With or without clothes? A video, doing it?

We spent most of the day filling things in and were pretty stressed out towards the end, and we'd barely made a mark. It was going to take weeks.

I drove us into Bankstown and we walked around. It was a hot night and people were on the streets and sitting in the outside cafés. Ekaterina was amazed at the different nationalities, Viets, Arabs, Africans, Indigenous, us Anglos, and the rest. It wasn't like that when I was a kid I told her. I asked if it was a problem. '*Nyeht*,' she said, shaking her head.

We got some Leb pizzas then went back home and turned on the TV. Ekaterina produced another bottle of vodka; she'd obviously bought up big on duty free, that's probably why the bag was so heavy at the airport. I think everyone in Russia drinks vodka like we drink water. I tried to remember the name of the Russian president who was drunk all the time. Ekaterina wouldn't tell me. She just shook her head. As a kid I'd watched him on TV, dancing and stumbling all over the place. I thought he was funny.

We watched *Australian Story*, to help Ekaterina learn more about the country. TV's a good way to learn English. Unless it's American.

I kept thinking about the night before. In fact, I'd thought about it all day. Ekaterina hadn't said anything, but I had had too much to drink. It would have spoiled things, our first real night together, and me drunk.

She sat close to me on the sofa. But she was tense. I could feel it.

I only had a couple of shots of vodka, I didn't want to end up drunk again. But she had a lot. I was edgy. I wondered if she always drank or whether it was because of the stress. Russian women are different, that's what all the websites said.

I took hold of her hand and she smiled. 'You ready for bed?' I asked.

I felt her stiffen. 'I cannot. Sorry.'

'Why the Christ not?' I regretted saying it like that, but it was out.

'It is the wrong time.'

It was my turn to apologise.

She downed another vodka and got up. 'Tomorrow we can do more the visa?'

Every day she was beginning to sound more like one of those Russian women on a British TV spy drama. A baddie.

'Yeah. Tomorrow.'

She leaned over and kissed me on the lips. '*Spah koy ni nochyee.* Goodnight,' and off she went into her room, leaving me on the sofa watching TV.

Ekaterina was very sweet next morning. She kissed me and gave me a little hug. She made breakfast for the first time; boiled eggs, and orypeu, cucumber and bread – she had done a bit of local shopping. After breakfast we got stuck into the visa application again. An absolute nightmare.

Questions.

Questions.

Questions.

Each one we answered led to a dozen more. But it was nice being so close to her again.

We worked on it all day. I'd had enough by lunchtime but Ekaterina insisted we keep going, even though she wasn't feeling too well. She's tough. By late afternoon, even she couldn't go on. I cooked an early dinner then she went straight to bed. I wasn't far behind. Me into my bed. She into hers.

It was the same the next day. And the day after. And the day after. Until finally we had everything filled in and lodged. All we had to do then was get on with our lives together for the next two years or so and hope that she was accepted.

*

I might not be the smartest guy in the world but even I worked out that things weren't exactly as Ekaterina had claimed.

She didn't like taking long walks.

She didn't like art galleries and museums.

But particularly, she didn't like me. I didn't light her fire. Her bedroom door was locked to me. Occasionally I heard her whispering on the phone.

One night we'd been sitting drinking vodka and watching TV. She'd gone to bed and I heard her talking. I hammered on the door until she opened it.

'Who ya talking to? You said ya had no one.'

'An old aunty in Russia.'

'An old aunty?' I wasn't gonna cop that one. 'Bullshit!'

She looked at me angrily. The scar on her nose flared. 'I tell you true'

'What's her name? Let me talk to her.' I reached for the phone.

'Speaks not English.'

'You translate,' I shouted.

'You have to trust me. Please. Don't be jealous.'

'Jealous! Jealous! Of your aunty?'

She shook her head. Her eyes filled with tears.

I grabbed her wrist. 'Show me the number.'

She held onto the phone like her life depended on it.

I had her by both wrists and twisted and a pulled and shoved as I fought to get the phone.

She would not let go.

We tumbled around the little bedroom, crashing into the walls, knocking over the bedside table, falling onto the bed then the floor, rolling around like two dogs snarling and fighting in the street.

We became a knot in which neither could move. I was on top, she was underneath, her face centimetres from mine, sweating, her blonde hair ragged as a witch, glaring up at me, hate in her eyes.

But she would not let go of that phone. Whatever number was there, Ekaterina was not going to let me to see it.

I gave in. I untangled myself and got to my feet. My legs and hands were shaking. I could scarcely breathe.

Ekaterina had her back to the wall. She was gasping for breath, her hands clutching the phone to her breasts, tears streaming down her face.

I turned and walked out.

She closed the door. I heard the bolt click.

So this was what Mum meant when she'd said, 'Women maketh the man.' What sort of a man had Ekaterina made me? A man who attacks a woman. A man who can't face the truth.

I'd been set up.

Used.

Taken for an idiot.

For what purpose?

I'm not so naive that I hadn't heard about such things; the Russian mafia, prostitution rings. All sorts of things. But Ekaterina didn't fit any of them. I had been patient, really patient. I knew it must have been hard to come to a country where you had no family, then get married to someone you didn't know. I think I was patient.

Maybe she did have an old aunty. How would I know?

I had really liked her when she arrived. I thought she was beautiful, her round, trusting face, her blonde hair. She'd awakened something in me that I didn't know was there. I'd started to love her. I'd thought her Russian accent cute, now I hated it. I thought the scar on her nose made her ugly. Her whole face was ugly. I hated her.

I know I'm not like most guys in some ways but was the problem with me, or was it with her? Or were we just incompatible?

Despite our fight, despite the phone calls, I tried to persuade her we should give it a go. We were man and wife; we should live as man and wife. But all she'd bloody well say was, *'Nyeht.'* Sometimes she was hard and defensive. Other times she cried.

She came up with what she thought was a solution. After breakfast one morning she said, 'I shop. I cook. I clean house. But not more.'

'I don't want a mother. I want a wife!' I yelled. What did she think I was? It was total humiliation.

She went white and the scar on her nose stood out in a red, ugly, crescent. Tears flowed. She shook her head.

What could I do? I thought about it over and over for the next few days. I could throw her out. She had no money, no friends, no job and nowhere to go. She'd be on the street. All sorts of things could happen: rape, murder, prostitution. And it would be my fault. What would other people think of me when they found out?

I could dob her in to Immigration. How embarrassing would that be. I'd have to explain to them that she wouldn't sleep with me. They'd deport her – for not letting me into her bed.

I could apply for an annulment of the marriage. What could I tell Alan and Mark? It would be all over the office in no time. 'Thomas the loser bought a Russian bride and she wouldn't even let him shag her.'

Kama-bloody-*Sutra*! Alan should get a refund.

Ekaterina was never going to love me. Maybe she never tried. Maybe she never wanted to. I'd bought her a ticket to an Australian fairyland, booked online, admit one. No refund. If I evicted her but didn't tell Immigration, they would find out. They snoop. Her permanent resident's visa would be denied, she'd be sent back to Mother Russia.

Good.

Not my problem.

I'd had enough. We stopped doing things together. We barely spoke. I'd go off to work. The guys stopped asking me stupid things like 'How's your Russian doll?' and 'Is she red in bed?'

She'd go a few evenings a week to a waitressing job she'd found at Bondi. Or so she said. But what was she really up to? We ate together occasionally. That was all. She was polite and tried to be nice. Of course, I was her lifeline and she knew that the rope was fraying.

This went on for a while as I thought things through.

Eventually I made a decision. One evening I turned up at the Bondi restaurant across from the beach and waited outside for her shift to finish. She emerged arm in arm – with a woman. Russian. I could tell.

They were smiling and laughing together. I followed them for a while at a distance as they walked along Campbell Parade past the shops and cafés. They looked very happy, like old friends. Then they stopped, put their arms around each other – and kissed. Passionately. Lips on lips. I couldn't believe what I was seeing. It was like being punched in the guts. I couldn't breathe. I thought I was never going to breathe again. I propped against a wall and hung on. Gradually my breathing got back to normal.

Ekaterina and the other one were still standing there, arms around each other's necks, foreheads touching, not worrying what anyone thought. And no one seemed to care but me. Ekaterina was one of those – a lesbian. Except Ekaterina didn't look like one.

I had thought for weeks that she had a guy, and that's what the secret phone calls were about. But a girlfriend? The thought never entered my mind. That it was a woman made the betrayal seem all that much worse somehow. I'd never thought much about sex between woman. Until now. I knew of course, like everyone else. But this, this was Ekaterina, my wife. With another woman.

It explained a whole lot of things, like why she wouldn't have sex with me. I'd thought all the time that it was just me, that there was something wrong with me, which there was, I guess, from Ekaterina's point of view.

I followed them as they crossed the road and walked down the hill past the pavilion and along the promenade above the beach. They hung on to each other's arms so they didn't get blown over. I didn't know what to do. I couldn't keep following them. It was decided for me. A southerly buster had sprung up during the afternoon and a particularly strong gust of wind barrelled in from the sea. The two women spun and turned their backs as they bent over to avoid the full force.

When they straightened, Ekaterina looked up and saw me. She froze. She was as surprised to see me as I had been surprised to see the two of them. She stood looking at me, her mouth open more than usual, showing those white teeth. She unhooked herself from the woman and came slowly towards me. She hesitated then said, 'Hello, Thomas.'

We stood and looked at each other for what seemed like forever. Then I told her I wanted to have a little walk on the beach with her.

She shook her head. '*Nyeht.*'

She was afraid I was going to drown her. The surf was huge, three to four metres. The whole bay was white water, surging up the steep slope of the beach and dragging back out, again and again. No one could last long in there. Eventually I persuaded her. She turned round to look at her friend then fell in alongside me. Sand whipped along at ankle height and the wind tried to pull the hair from her head.

'You are out of my place!' I shouted above the thunder of the surf. 'As from now.'

Earlier that afternoon when she was at work I had emptied her room and packed her clothes and other things. Regardless of what I'd found,

I didn't want her around at all. The bags were sitting in the back of the car parked above the beach on Campbell Parade. One of the bags had an envelope with five hundred dollars. A farewell present to my Russian bride. I'd changed the locks on the house. This worm had turned.

After a short distance, Ekaterina stopped. I walked a few more metres then I stopped too and looked round. Down the beach, almost hidden by blowing sand and the growing dark, I could see the vague shape of Ekaterina's lover, following us. The three of us were the only people on the long curve of beach.

I was ready for Ekaterina's tears, anger, or pleading.

Instead she was very calm. 'Please. I explain. Come,' she said.

She took hold of my arm and tried to lead me from the beach but I shook her off.

'Coffee. We talk,' she begged.

That was a bit rich. 'You stopped talking to me ages ago.'

'Please.' She turned her face towards me imploringly.

It was a lovely face and I was angry with myself for still thinking that it was a lovely face.

'Nah!' I shook my head. What did she think I was?

'Please, listen.' She hung on to my sleeve. 'I'm sorry, I was bad to you. Everything was for me, nothing you. I left Russia for love, but another person.'

'Her!' I jerked my head back down the beach.

Ekaterina nodded. 'She in Sydney two years. Not legal. We were together in Moscow.'

'She's the old aunty you kept phoning?'

Ekaterina nodded. I couldn't believe what I was hearing. My legs wouldn't hold me. I sank to the sand and sat there, knees pointing to the dark sky, my hands covering my head. All along I had thought there was a guy on the other end of the phone. Why hadn't she told me the truth? Why hadn't she trusted me?

Ekaterina knelt by me and put a hand on my shoulder. 'Sorry hurt you. Really sorry.'

She was silent for a while. But stood there, her hand still on my shoulder. I hadn't the strength to push it away.

'I had to escape to Australia to join her.'

I looked up into her face. 'Why pick me? Why not some other idiot?'

'Not an idiot. You kind, that's why I pick you.'

She was silent for while, like she was waiting for me to absorb what she was saying.

'In Russia, women with women are hated.' She touched the scar on her nose. 'We were together. They pull us from bed. They beat. She nearly die. In Russia we criminals. No, what you call, civil right. Government stop all gay protest.' She spat out the word government.

Of all the things I thought might have been going on with Ekaterina, I could never have come up with this.

'Why couldn't I have found a normal Russian woman? Why you?'

'It was me who found you,' she said.

Why of all the women available on the world's dating sites did I choose this one?

'Thomas…'

I struggled to my feet and tried to brush off the sand. She took my hand. She is still lovely. I hate myself for thinking that.

We walked, a few metres apart, back up the beach towards the promenade. I could no longer see the other woman.

Before I drove back to Bankstown, I gave Ekaterina a new key. When I got home, I put her clothes and other things back in her room, Mum's old room.

I kept the money. I let her stay on.

She eventually got a full-time job in the Bondi restaurant. She went to English classes. She is going to become a teacher like back home. We became friends, at a distance, but I couldn't forgive her for what she had done.

The day her permanent resident visa arrived, she left the house and moved in with her lover. I never asked the woman's name. I didn't want to know anything about her. I didn't want Immigration or Border Control sniffing around me, getting information. She remained the distant figure on the beach.

I never saw them again.

I sometimes wonder what it is like living with someone who at any moment could be arrested and deported. Your world would collapse overnight. Ekaterina must love her a lot.

I'm going out with a woman I met through an online dating site. Her name's Yasmin. She lives in Bankstown. We have lots of things in common and plan to get married when my divorce comes through.

When I was cleaning out Ekaterina's room, I found a gift-wrapped box with my name on it. Inside were two shot glasses with the head of a man engraved on each; the former Soviet president, Boris Yeltsin. Now I remembered – he was the one who was always drunk on TV.

I also found the thong-shaped dip bowl that Mark and Sophie had given us, tucked away at the back of the drawer. They had slipped a business card for a divorce lawyer in the box. Great to have friends with a sense of humour.

I'd kept the *Kama Sutra*. I'm glad I did.

Comfort Zone

Sometimes my dad's more trouble than he's worth. Like the time we went camping way out in the bush.

Mum was against the idea. 'It's going to rain. Let's stay in a motel,' she said as we turned off the highway.

'The forecast's only for showers,' Dad told her.

'Showers are still wet,' Mum countered.

'There's a drought, global warming and all that,' Dad said.

He's real stubborn sometimes.

They argued. Dad won. A pity. We drove along this track across paddocks for kilometres. 'A field road,' Dad called it. I opening and closed all the gates – thirteen of them, jumping in and out of the car in the drizzly rain.

Dad chose a place to camp on a little flat patch at the edge of the forest. Mum and me attached a flysheet to the back of the station wagon and unrolled our swags under it on the wet grass while Dad used dry kindling from the car to get a fire going. Mum was right about the weather. The rain was heavier.

'It'll soon pass. It's only a shower,' Dad said.

I think that sort of thing's called ignoring reality.

He stood holding his yellow plastic cape over the flames to keep the rain off while he grilled steaks. The fire hissed and the grill sizzled. Dad danced around it in some weird corroboree trying to avoid the smoke going under the bottom of his cape and out at the neck. My dad doesn't give up.

'This is great, Dad,' I called out.

He waved, and blinked and coughed. Mum made a 'humph' noise. She crouched under the flysheet, cooking the vegies on a stove.

Frogs started croaking in a little pond near the tent. I hadn't noticed the pond before.

Eventually Dad took the cooked meat off the spitting grill and brought it over to the shelter of the flysheet. Mum dished out the rest of the dinner and we ate crouched in our chairs trying to avoid the dripping water. I had to admit it tasted fantastic. Rain adds a great flavour to mashed potatoes.

'It's good to get out of your comfort zone once in a while,' Dad mumbled through a mouthful.

'Why?' Mum and me chorused.

I could have been dry at home watching TV or doing stuff with my mates. 'What's wrong with being comfortable, Dad?'

'We're seeing nature in all its moods, Brett. Humans are too used to controlling everything,' Dad said. He should have been a teacher instead of an air con mechanic.

The fire was no longer spitting and hissing – it was out.

I thought I could hear thunder. 'Did you hear it?' I asked Mum.

'It's the wind,' Dad said.

'It wasn't windy when we stopped,' Mum pointed out.

She was right. Water was now shaking in sheets from the trees on the other side of the clearing.

'It'll soon pass,' Dad said, wrapping his hands around his mug and sipping his tea.

It didn't. The rain got heavier. I shone my head torch into the darkness. The pale finger of light reached the pond. I hadn't realised how big it was. Rain bounced off its surface.

I thought again of what I could have been doing instead of huddling under a flysheet in a forest with my mum and dad listening to rain rattle down. Not riveting entertainment.

'What about the kayaking we were gonna do, Dad?'

'Tomorrow, if there's not too much water in the river.'

Mum pounced. 'Oh! So it might keep on raining!'

Dad ignored her.

'I'm goin' ta bed,' I told them.

'Me too,' said Mum.

'And me,' Dad added.

I wriggled into my sleeping bag, switched on my head torch and got my book. Within minutes, I was lovely and warm. But I couldn't read. There seemed to be hundreds of frogs croaking in the pond. Rain rattled on the fly and poured like a waterfall from trees across the clearing.

I might have dropped off to sleep once or twice. I'm not sure. But I don't think Mum or Dad did. There was none of that rhythmic breathing. All I could hear was water and wind. Even the frogs had stopped croaking.

I was slipping into sleep, half dream, half real, when I heard a great swishing sound above my head, then an enormous thump. The ground shook. Like an elephant had dropped from the sky. That was no dream.

'Whatwasthat?' Mum screamed.

We wriggled free of our sleeping bags, colliding with each other as we dragged on rain gear and switched on our torches.

We peered into the rain.

An enormous dead tree trunk lay in front of the car, right against the bumper bar. It hadn't been there when we parked. We stood gaping, side by side, three people, one thought. A bit closer and we would have been burger meat. Pinned to the ground where no one would have found us for months. Or years.

I felt sick. And I felt wet. I looked down where my feet should have been. Water was swirling around my calves. The pond was a lake. Our sleeping bags were floating.

Dad reached into the car and switched on the headlights. Through the white rods of driving rain we could see the huge fallen tree reaching way back into the bush. We stood and gaped. My guts knotted into a fist.

'Let's go!' Dad yelled.

I scooped up the soggy sleeping bags and flung them into the back of the wagon while Dad and Mum pulled down the fly and grabbed the cooking things.

The track we had driven in on was a river. No way out there.

I splashed around looking for a space we could drive back onto the track. My head torch poked the dark and rain. I spotted an area above water and clear of scrub. 'Reverse in there!' I shouted and pointed.

I started to tell Dad he could get back onto the track nose-first, but he had already got it, and scrambled into the driving seat. Mum and me ran in front to make sure there were no deep holes full of water. Dad drove slowly into the driving rain.

I could smell exhaust fumes and burning rubber as he skidded behind us. I was sure any minute he'd get bogged.

He kept going, bottom gear, engine roaring. We were almost out when the front wheels hit something. Mud and water sprayed all over Mum and me as we shoved and heaved from the back. The car was stuck. The rain pelted down. Water was up to our knees.

I knelt by the front wheels and thrust my arms under, trying to keep my head above water. My fingers closed on a log. I pulled. It didn't budge.

Mum knelt besides me, her hair plastered against her face, her hood thrown back. We pulled and pushed but the log wouldn't shift.

Dad leaned out the window and waved us away from the car then reversed. He jumped out and the three of us fumbled in the rushing water until we found the log. It was stuck in the mud and wanted to stay there. We pulled and tugged until it came free and we dragged it to one side.

Dad thrust Mum into the driver's seat and him and me got behind and shoved like our lives depended on it. They probably did.

The car crept forwards until the front wheels bit into hard gravel and lurched onto the forest road.

We were out, out of that place anyway. But not out of the woods yet. Dad drove, as fast as he dared – all of us thinking, if one waterlogged dead tree could come down, so could others. We skirted fallen branches and splashed through dark pools in the road.

Finally we were clear of the trees and out in open paddocks. I was gate-opener again. But this time I didn't count. I was just glad to be in the clear. The only thing we had to worry about now were the creeks we had to cross. At each one, muddy water swirled around the hubcaps. But it didn't come higher. The three of us breathed with relief when we crossed the last creek.

Dad pulled the car over at the top of a hill, well away from water and trees. He yanked the handbrake on so hard I thought it would come off in his hand. 'Wow, what an adventure, eh!'

Neither Mum nor I answered.

We covered ourselves in towels and what dry clothes we could find, and tried to make ourselves comfortable.

'Put the radio on. We might catch the weather forecast,' Dad said.

'You gotta be joking,' Mum told him, and turned on her side.

Rain pounded the roof and condensation from three hot, wet bodies trickled down the inside of the windows like an arty installation. There was nothing to see outside but black night and the faint shape of paddocks.

I must have fallen asleep because the next thing was grey dawn at the windows. I wiped the back of my hand against the cold glass. We were on a grassy hillock.

The drought's over. Does that mean global warming's finished?

A huge pink thing slid up the glass. I recoiled and tried to retreat into the car but there was no room to move. It came again, big and slimy, like a skinned snake.

I peered out.

A cow looked in. Her tongue came up once more and licked the rain from the glass. Big eyes focused on through drizzling rain as though to ask, 'What you doing here?'

'Ask my dad,' I said out loud.

'What's that?' Mum muttered in her sleep.

'Just a shower,' Dad mumbled, and kept on snoring.

North Head

Between sobs, the woman tells them her name is Crystal.

Moments ago, Amy and Bill were walking quietly along the narrow bush track from the cliffs back to the little car park. They had been looking down on the sparkling ocean, a hundred metres below yellow sandstone cliffs. They'd watched a sea eagle riding a thermal, gannets diving – white arrows into blue sea. The faint smell of heathland plants hung on the cool autumn air.

Then this.

A jeep had crunched to a halt as they were about to get into their car.

A woman screamed from its open window, 'He's gonna throw me off the cliff!' She'd jumped out, run across to them and grabbed Bill by his arm, repeating in a pleading voice, 'He's gonna throw me off.'

For a moment, Amy and Bill are transfixed. Then Amy takes hold of Crystal's hands to calm her. Crystal's face is full of confusion and fear.

'It's OK,' Amy says. Even though she's not sure it is.

The jeep moves away, slowly, a leisurely crunching of tyres. The windows are tinted. It's not possible to see the driver, even whether there is a driver. Bill tries to memorise the number plate but the car disappears round a bend in the track.

Crystal is sobbing, clinging to Amy's hands, repeating what she has already said, over and over.

'You're safe with us,' Amy tells her, glancing down the track in the direction of the disappeared jeep, then at Bill for reassurance.

Crystal nods. She wipes tears from her cheek with the back of her hand then takes hold of Amy again. She is in her early thirties, dark hair, pretty, wearing tights, runners and a light fleece jacket.

'My brother. Hunter. He said. He's gonna. Kill me.' She speaks in fractured gasps.

'Brother?' Amy and Bill say in unison. They look at each other in disbelief.

Crystal, sensing their confusion, says. 'He's threatened before. He hates me.'

Bill digs in the pocket of his jeans for his phone. 'I'll get the police.'

'Don't.' Crystal shakes her head. 'Please.'

'Why?' Bill asks incredulously.

Crystal shakes her head again and says, 'No. Please, no, I want to go home.'

Amy asks where that is.

'Menai.' Crystal names a suburb south-west of the city.

'What about him, your brother?' Bill asks.

'I asked him to bring me here.'

'Asked?' Amy says, not sure she is hearing correctly.

'I didn't think that…'

'I don't understand,' Bill says.

'He said OK. Then he said he'd throw me into the sea.'

'Are you sure?' Amy asks. She tries to keep her voice soft and reassuring.

Crystal nods.

'So, where's he gone?'

'I don't know,' Crystal tells them.

'He might come back. I should call the cops,' Bill says.

'Is there anyone else at home?' Amy asks.

'Him. Me. No, don't. He wants to kill me.'

'Why?' Amy repeats their question.

'He hates me. He's always hated me. Mum and Dad will back me up.'

'Where are they?' Amy asks.

'Somewhere.'

'Can't you contact them?'

Crystal ignores the question.

'Have you no one else? Boyfriend? Husband? Other brothers? Sisters? Friends?' Amy asks.

Crystal shakes her head. She is no longer crying. 'I want to go home.'

'Won't your brother be there?' Bill asks.

'No, he brings me here.'

'He's tried to kill you before? And you still come?' Bill is trying to get his head around what is happening. 'Why haven't you told the police?'

'They don't believe me.'

Amy holds Crystal's hands and looks into her face. It is waxen. Wrinkles invade the corners of her eyes. 'They know? Then why don't they arrest him?' Amy asks.

Crystal shakes her head.

'And you still want to go home? Do you have money?' Bill asks.

Crystal answers both questions with a nod. 'Will you take me to the ferry?'

The three of them walk to the car. Amy takes Crystal's hands and holds them in her lap as they sit in the back seat.

Bill drives slowly out of the car park. At the first bend, the jeep is blocking the road. The driver's window slides slowly down.

Crystal squeezes closer to Amy.

Bill locks the doors. The driver of the jeep looks at him with hooded eyes. He is a man of about forty, balding, thin-faced. 'Has she asked you to fuck her yet?'

The window begins to slowly close.

'You don't know what you're letting yourselves in for, she's an alcoholic – among other things,' he adds, as his face disappears behind the dark glass.

Bill turns to look at Crystal. She is crying again.

'Well?' he says.

She tells him again that she wants to go home.

Amy screws up her mouth, raises and drops her shoulders in a gesture of, what should we do? Bill sits for a moment then drives slowly away. He half expects the jeep to be waiting around each corner but the road is deserted. He takes Amy and Crystal to the Manly ferry wharf. It feels safer there.

'I'll get us something to eat.' He leaves them without waiting for a response and drives around the corner. He finds a parking spot, and fishes in his pocket for his mobile.

At the wharf, Amy and Crystal sit silently side by side in the sun as the tide of tourists flows in and out from the ferries. Amy wonders where the truth lies.

Eventually Crystal says, 'I'm pregnant.'

Amy doesn't respond for some time, then she asks, 'Does the father know?'

'Which?'

'Which what?'

'Which father?'

'You mean you don't know?'

Crystal doesn't answer.

'How long?'

'A month.'

'What are you going to do?'

Crystal shrugs. 'I wish I had a mother like you. Can you be my mother?'

'It's not that easy.'

'Hunter won't face up to his problems.'

Amy lowers her head and peers at Crystal over the rim of her glasses, waiting for more.

'He was molested as a child.'

Amy doesn't ask, by whom?

'If that's true...'

'Of course it's true.'

'What's that got to do with him wanting to kill you? How would that help him?'

'Ask him.'

'He's not here.'

'He was.'

'Why does he want to kill you?'

'I want to go home.'

'That won't be a safe place if he wants to kill you.'

The more Amy says, the less sense it makes. Yet what if Hunter is trying to kill her and their being at North Head prevented it – this time?

'You said he's taken you to North Head before. If you're frightened, why come?'

'He made me.'

'He forced you into the car?'

'He made me. He had a wife once. Angela. She was so demanding. Never left him alone. She wanted his attention all the time. Me. Me. Me.'

Amy wishes Bill would hurry.

'He never had any time for his little sister. Even when I went to live with them, it was the same. He was my big brother then she came along. Angela this and Angela that. No time for me. Even my boyfriends couldn't stand her. A couple of weeks and they were off.' Crystal stands impatiently. 'I'm going home.'

'Won't he be there?'

'Who? Ah, him. I don't know, do I?' Crystal walks towards the entrance to the ferry.

Amy follows. 'Wait till Bill's back, we'll have a bite to eat, then sort something out,' she calls after her.

Crystal stops, scrabbles around in her bag like a dog in a flowerbed and produces an Opal card. She taps it at the barrier but the gate doesn't open. She taps again. Still nothing. She stands in hopeless frustration.

'Just wait a bit longer,' Amy pleads.

Crystal looks around for help and a ferry attendant comes across.

'Back again,' he says.

Crystal smiles.

He opens the gate and lets her through.

Crystal turns towards Amy and gives her a little wave. 'Thanks for rescuing me.'

'Had the baby yet?' the ferry man says as Crystal walks past.

'You know her?' Amy asks in disbelief.

He shakes his head, more to himself than to her. 'Yeah, she turns up every few months. Usually with a guy, her brother.'

Amy watches Crystal disappears on board. The gangplanks are drawn in. White water churns from the stern as the ferry ploughs into the harbour.

As she retraces her steps along the jetty, Amy becomes aware of people watching an ambulance parked on the footpath. Bill is next to it, talking earnestly to a policewoman and looking around for her.

The Chicken

The day was hot. The passengers on the minibus that bounced along the dry stony road towards the distant brown of Morocco's High Atlas Mountains were nodding off. Their necks flicked back and forth as they slipped in and out of restless sleep.

Youssef turned his slight figure around from his position next to the driver and looked at his drowsy charges. They had not come halfway around the world to sleep in a minibus. I have a story for you, he said. He waited.

Youssef the guide was famous for his stories. They were like tales from the Arabian Nights. They were not to be missed. Often they were funny.

The sleepers awoke one by one. He waited a little longer. Timing, as all storytellers know, is as important as words.

When I was old enough to go high school, I had to leave my village in the mountains because there was no school there, Youssef said.

He paused and smiled to make sure he had everyone's attention.

There were ten of us in the family. My parents could afford to educate only one, me. I was thirteen, the youngest. I wanted to learn and I was excited to be going live in the big city of Marrakech.

Youssef paused and smiled again. The eyes and ears of the ten tourists were on him.

An aunty I had never met offered to let me stay with her family while I was at high school. On the day I left, all my family and friends came to say goodbye. My father gave me ten dirham for food on the journey. He and my brothers hugged me and my mother and three sisters cried. I pretended to cry too and managed to squeeze out a few little tears but really I was so glad to go. So excited. I was happy. I was leaving my village for the first time. I was the lucky one. But I was frightened too.

Youssef grinned at the tourists. They nodded, understanding, and waited for what was next.

I had two bags with me. One had my personal things. The other held a live chicken, a gift from my mother to my aunty. The driver told me I had to pay five dirham for each bag. Ten dirham! That was the money for food for the whole journey. I did not want to ask my father for more. I already felt I was independent, a man

I tried to argue with the driver. But I was very small for my age and he was very big for any age. He held out his hand. More, he demanded. I thought of my ten dirham and of the chicken and of my aunty. I did not want to part with even one dirham. So I gave the driver one of the bags, paid five dirham, and when he wasn't looking, I smuggled the one with the chicken onto the crowded bus.

I squeezed onto a seat next to a man with a thin, lined face, a poor farmer, like my father. I hid the silent chicken under the seat. As I did, I noticed the man also had a bag under his seat, hidden by his djellaba, those baggy, ankle length smocks that people of my country wear. He smiled at me in a funny way, and the bus set off down the windy, bumpy road.

We stopped at other villages to pick up more passengers, more luggage. The driver was a bad-tempered man who didn't like anyone in the world. Maybe he had a pain in his belly all the time. I watched as he counted the things each person was putting on the roof and bringing onto the bus and held out his hand for money. I was pleased with myself for hiding one off my bags and saving five dirham, but at the same time I was scared the chicken might make a noise and the driver would find it. Then what?

It was a long journey. The chicken must be hungry by now. I hoped that it had just closed its eyes in the dark the way chickens do, and would stay asleep.

The man next to me sat looking straight ahead. Occasionally he touched his bag under the seat behind his djellaba, as though making sure it was still there. Then he would give that strange smile he had. But he never spoke.

The seat was hard and my bum ached. The bus bumped its way down the twisting, narrow, mountain roads, then past the little farms along the banks of the shallow, rocky river where the snow-melt milky water flooded in spring. The journey seemed to go on forever.

Eventually we stopped so we could get something to eat. The other passengers got off the bus. I waited till the driver had walked away to have a pee, then I climbed down too, but the man next to stayed where he was, all by himself.

I could see the blue smoke from the barbecue fires and smell lamb kebabs cooking. I was so hungry. I spent my last five dirham. Then I got back on the bus as quickly as I could before the driver. The man next to me was still there. He smiled his thin smile and ran a finger across his little moustache. Maybe he had brought food with him. Maybe that's what was under the seat behind the djellaba.

The bad-tempered driver clambered back into his seat and started the engine. He blasted the horn and the last of the passengers hurried back. The driver stood up and turned around to check we were all on. I'm sure he glared at me. He clunked into gear and the bus bumped back onto the road.

The driver was in a hurry now and the bus swayed around the corners without slowing. He wasn't worried about donkeys, or cars, or trucks getting in the way.

What would happen if my chicken woke up and start to cluck? I had no money left. Would the driver throw me off the bus in the middle of nowhere?

As we reached the outer suburbs of Marrakech, I could hear the chicken shuffling around. It clucked. My neighbour looked at me and raised an eyebrow. The skin stretched tight over his thin cheekbones as he smiled.

I whispered to the chicken to be quiet. It ignored me and clucked again, frantically now. Then it started to jump up and down, trying to get out. I could feel its wings flapping against my legs.

The driver of the bus looked through his rear-view mirror. He had heard the commotion. He pulled the bus off the road and started walking down the aisle, stepping over the clutter of boxes and bags, checking every passenger, glaring through red-rimmed eyes. I pretended to be asleep. He drew level, and stopped. The chicken flapped and clucked loudly.

I kept my eyes shut.

The bus driver tapped the top of my head. Off! he said.

I opened my eyes and looked up at him. He was very big and very angry. He jerked his thumb in the direction of the door. Off. Or pay. Five dirham.

I told him I couldn't. I pleaded with him. He shook his head. He went back to the driver's seat and sat there with the door open, waiting. We were a long, long way from the bus terminal where my aunty was going to meet me. Marrakech is a big city and I had never been in a big city before. I had never seen so many buildings, so many vehicles, so many people.

I stayed where I was. I was frightened of the driver, but I was even more frightened of getting off.

Everyone in the bus was watching, waiting to see what would happen.

The driver kept looking at me through the rear-view mirror. Finally he got up and walked back down the bus to me, stepping over the boxes and bags again like a man trying to dance. But he didn't look as angry now. You can stay on – if you give me the chicken, he said.

The chicken was for my aunty, from my mother. My aunty was going to look after me. My mother wanted her to be happy about it. I shook my head and gripped the handles of the bag. The chicken clucked even louder and scratched and flapped.

The driver stood, one hand on the seat above my head, the other on his hip. My passengers are waiting. They are tired.

I shook my head. I can't.

The driver glared down at me.

Then, the man next to me spoke for the first time. He is only a boy. It is only a chicken, he said, looking the driver in the eyes.

The driver looked around at the other passengers. They were being held up, almost at their destination. He sensed whose side they were on. He glared at me. He was so angry. But he turned and went back to his seat. He started the engine and pulled onto the road.

The man next to me smiled. He bent slowly over his bag. He opened it. Inside, was a baby. The man held a finger to his lips. It was our secret.

Youssef paused for effect, then grinned his big boyish grin.

The tourists let out a collective Ahhhh, then began to applaud.

(With thanks to Khalid Lamlih)

The Buoy

Waves lick Ben's legs and gently slap the stern of the tinny as he eases it into the water. His father cranks the winch on the trailer and the runabout slides further into the river. Ben holds the gunwale to stop it drifting.

His father unhooks the winch and drives the trailer off the concrete boat ramp, and crunches across the blue metal gravel into the car park. Ben watches him place the sun reflector behind the windscreen. He wishes he'd hurry. He can feel the tug of the little boat on the line, like a horse wanting to be off. His father wanders back in his shambling walk, picks up the esky from the pile of gear they have unloaded at the top of the ramp and carries it down to the boat. He wades into the water and heaves it aboard. He loads two rods, one of them new, a birthday present for Ben, the five-gallon white plastic sea anchor bucket, the tackle box, oars, the bag with waterproofs, two lifejackets, and the rest.

He grins at Ben. 'Nearly there.'

Ben steadies the boat as his father steps in and plants his big brown feet on the deck then begins stowing the gear in place.

Sand whiting in the river, maybe flathead, bream, his father has promised. Only the biggest and the best for tonight's barbecue.

'What if we don't get any?' Ben asks.

'Don't even think about it. Do I ever come home without anything?'

'Yeah.'

'Not often, though.'

'Sometimes you buy fish from the cooperative. Mum doesn't know.'

'That's a lie. Who told you that? Uncle Tom, I'll bet.'

Ben grins.

When everything is the way he wants, Ben's father looks at his son standing knee-deep in the water, 'Righto, buddy, in ya get.'

Ben swings one leg into the boat and pushes off with the other while his father grasps him by the wrist and pulls him aboard. As they drift slowly into the current, his father lowers the outboard, locks it into position and settles himself at the stern. He pulls the starter, once, twice, and the motor coughs into life. He takes the tiller in his hand and eases the little boat away from the ramp. With his big tattooed arms, his unshaven chin and his fishing knife at his waist, he reminds Ben of a pirate, a slightly chubby one, but a pirate. His mum says the tats look more like graffiti. That doesn't worry his dad. He just laughs it off and tells her to get her own.

Ben passes a lifejacket to his father and puts the other one on himself. His father jiggles his arms into the jacket as he steers the boat further out into the estuary then slips a phone from his shirt pocket and puts it to his ear. 'It's me, Angie, we're just heading out into the river. Perfect day... Of course we will.'

Ben makes a gesture to him which his father translates into 'Birthday boy wants to know have you started making the cake yet?' then he throws back his head and laughs. 'I'll tell him... Your mother says she's too tired to bother.'

Ben dips his hand into the river and flicks water over his father. He knows his mother better than that.

'We'll get an extra slab on the way home. Your Tom's coming, don't forget. He loves his beer,' his father says into the phone, smiling to himself. He momentarily holds it away from his ear with a mock grimace to Ben. 'Yeah, me too. Yeah, we'll be back early. How many times I have to tell ya? There'll be enough for the whole street,' he says. He slips the phone back into his pocket. 'A real worrier, your mum. "Stay in the river. Don't go over the bar. Keep you eyes on the weather. Make sure you've got your life jackets on. Look after Ben." You'd think I've never been out in a boat before. You'd think neither of us can swim.'

Ben waits for the story of how when his dad was a surf lifesaver he'd rescued three people in one day. But the story doesn't come. Today he is thinking fish!

They chug over the wide expanse of mud flats towards the deeper channel of the river, moving slowly against the current. There is a smell of mangroves warming in the early sun, and the tang of sea, borne on the incoming tide. Ben watches a flight of pelicans glide towards them low over the river, barely moving wings balancing their great white bodies on the air currents.

Ben's dad cuts the outboard. There is silence except for the chaffing water on the side of the tinny.

'Chuck the anchor in, mate,' his father tells him.

Ben drops the bucket into the river. It fills and sinks quickly. The line tightens, angles hard, and drops of water are catapulted into the air.

'What we using, Dad? Worms?'

'Yeah. We'll try for whiting.'

Ben baits the hooks. He watches as his father casts and plays out the bait into the water. He picks up his own rod and casts. The bait plops into the water a few metres away and Ben mutters in frustration.

'You weren't swearing, were ya?' His dad laughs.

Ben ignores him. He concentrates on reeling in the bait then casting again. It's better.

'Let it play out, then reel it in slowly,' his father instructs. 'Like this.'

Ben watches his father, then does the same.

They sit in silence, man and boy. Cast. Reel in. Cast. Reel in. Cast, watch the incoming tide carry their bait away from the boat and up river.

As the mudflats and sandbanks are inundated, the birds of the estuary, herons, pelicans, ibis and the small waders, take wing. Neither father nor son feel the need to talk. They sit, and savour the sound of the water and the restless birds.

No other boats are on the river. Autumn storms have visited early and the summer tourists have gone. Locals don't come out much midweek. Ben's dad has taken a day off to spend with his son on his birthday. People can unblock their own toilets.

The truth is that Ben is not keen on fishing – nor fish. But he wants to please his father as much as his father wants to please him.

After half an hour, they have caught nothing. Ben is restless and keeps reeling in to check the bait's still there.

'We'll try somewhere else,' his father says.

Ben nods. His father lays down his rod and moves to pull in the bucket anchor.

'I'll do it.' Ben grabs the line. His arms are slight, the bucket is heavy. He draws it slowly in, the line hard and wet in his hands. The bucket comes up from the dark water, white as a rising moon. Ben empties the water out and drops the bucket on board.

His father starts up the outboard and turns the tinny, leaving a white question mark wake in the water behind them. The roar of the engine drowns out the sound of everything but the slow bump, bump of the boat on the waves as they head towards the mouth of the river.

After a few hundred metres, Ben's father cuts the engine. Ben drops the bucket over the side and watches as it is caught by the tide, sinks and drags. The line is tight and the boat swings in an arc, pointing up river, rocking gently. Now the outboard is silenced, they can hear the muffled roar of surf at the bar.

'We'll try lures,' Ben's father says.

Ben opens the tackle box and looks at the array of lures arranged in their compartments. They will flash silver light and rainbows as they spin through the water, saying take me, take me. Ben wonders what a fish thinks when its breakfast grabs it by the throat. The hunter captured by its prey.

'Which ones, Dad?' he asks.

'The little ones, there on the right. We'll get a few flathead to start with.'

Ben slides the box across the boat and his father selects a plastic lure that looks more like a jelly baby than a fish. Ben ties a different lure on his line. He thinks that trying to guess what a fish wants for its dinner is like trying to guess what video game it would like to play.

They fish from the fretting boat. Man and boy cast and watch the angle of their lines as the lures are taken up river towards the hills. It is not as comfortable here. The current is strong where sea and river have cut a deep narrow channel along which the tide is sweeping. They can hear the surf loud now.

They cast and reel in. Cast and reel in. They change lures. None of the fish want what is being offered.

Ben's father tells him to pull in the sea anchor again. Ben draws the line in, hand over hand. It is harder this time in the stronger current but Ben wants to show his father that he can handle it.

When the bucket is clear of the surface, emptied and on board, they chug around the curve of the river. Closer to the sea, the land has drawn in on each side. The river channel is narrower and deeper. They can see the breakwater at the mouth of the bar, the two lines of black boulders stacked on black boulders, jutting into the ocean, directing the mouth of the river over the bar into the Pacific. When it is calm, like today, river and sea come together without too much quarrelling. Other days, the meeting is a place of enormous turmoil and conflict. Brown floodwaters sweeping down from the hills bring downed trees, drowned cattle and sheep. Occasionally a human. The dark mass of the flood river and the seething white cyclonic swells hit each other like two armies head on. Ben has stood in storms with his father and mother at the end of the breakwater watching over a sea that is the colour of mud as far as the horizon. Today is not such a day.

Ben's father cuts the outboard and Ben drops the bucket over the side. They cast and let their lines spin out in the fast moving water. They repeat what they have been doing, with the same results.

'They reckon that the fish in this river are the canniest in the state,' Ben's dad tells him as he once more reels in his empty lure.

'Who's "they"?' Ben asks.

'They are people who can't catch fish.'

Ben hides a mock grin with his hand.

'Unlike us, who are gonna catch a boatload,' his father continues.

They fish a while longer, with no luck.

Ben wonders what it is about fishing that people like. His dad for instance, who thinks there is something wrong with people who don't like it.

'What say we try the ocean?' His father suggests.

Ben looks up from watching the swirling water. 'Is it safe to cross the bar?'

'There's not much of a swell. Pick our time. It'll be right. We'll catch nothing here.'

Offshore could be fun. Something for Ben to tell Alex and Luke who don't go fishing with their dads.

'OK. Then we won't have to go to the co-op on the way home.'

'Smart arse.' Ben's father pulls his phone from his shirt pocket while Ben reels in. 'Angie, yeah me…an' you. Nothing's doing in the river, though. We're gonna go out a bit…coupla k at most. Yeah, I know what I said but it's a waste of time here… Settle down, will ya?'

Ben stops reeling, waits, then lets the lure run out again as his father sits, phone in one hand, rod in the other.

'It's like a millpond,' his father says eventually. 'I know… Stop worrying. We'll be back in time.' He slips the phone into his pocket. 'She goes on a bit at times, your mum.'

He reels in. Ben does the same. His father starts up the outboard and they swing the tinny in the direction of the bar and open sea. The breeze from the speeding boat is cooling. Ben dips his hand in the water and splashes his legs and feet. It's going to be hot. He pulls his cap tighter over his forehead.

His father's eyes are on the narrow channel across the bar between the breakwaters. White water chews at the rocks on each side. He noses the boat in the direction of the deeper dark channel where the swell rolls in.

The bow lifts and thumps down and a few seconds later lifts and thumps again. Ben's stomach knots and he holds tight to the gunwale. He knows things can go wrong, even on a calm day, going out, or coming in. Boats can be suddenly upended by a misjudged rogue wave or some surge from below. Usually people are saved by the coastguard. Not always.

His father grins at him, delighting in the swell and the noise of water breaking on the rocks. He finds an outgoing rip, steers into it and momentarily opens the throttle before the next wave rolls in through the mouth.

Within minutes, they are clear of the bar and breakwaters. In front, the blue curved skin of the Pacific extends to the horizon. Behind, and to the north and south of the bar, waves roll onto white beaches like lines of horses. Ben will be there tomorrow with his new boogie board, a birthday present from his mum, celebrating with Alex and Luke.

They head out to sea. Eventually Ben's father slows the engine. The boat rises and falls gently in the swell.

'This'll do,' he says.

Ben throws the bucket over the side and it disappears into the dark water where there are millions of fish. How many are looking up at the underside of the little boat waiting to be fed? Ben hopes there are loads.

Father and son cast. The mouth of the river is just visible, a dark break in the white line of surf.

'We'll catch something big here for sure,' his dad says.

Ben opens the esky, hands a bottle of water to his father and takes one himself. He rubs the cold bottle along the back of his neck before taking a long drink. He takes out sandwiches and they sit munching and looking at the sea. A swell from the east is picking up.

'Twelve years old, eh Ben. Feel any different to yesterday?' his dad says.

'Yeah. A year older. Catching up on ya.'

'Long way to go yet, mate. A long way.'

'I'm moving faster than you, though.'

'How do you work that out?'

'Well, in one year I increased my age almost ten per cent. You were thirty-nine last year, right? On your next birthday you'll have increased your age by only two-and-a-half per cent. So, I'm catching up.'

'Well, whoda thought.' His father is not sure whether Ben is serious or not. He's a funny kid. Thinks differently. Must get it from his mum. 'Decided what you wanta to do when you leave school? Plumber like me? Brain surgeon?'

'No, I'm gonna make loadsa money – fishing.'

They both laugh.

'I promised your mum we'd get enough to feed everybody.'

'What's gone wrong?'

'You never give up when you're fishing. We'll go out a bit further.'

The motor coughs into life and they head further out until they can see only the coast range, a barely visible, thin, dark line.

Ben's father cuts the engine and they drift on the sea anchor. The sun is no longer overhead but the day is still hot.

'How's the rod?' Ben's father asks.

'Great.'

'You like it, eh?'

'Yeah.'

'I knew ya would. I'll bet you'd get to like fishing as much as me.'

Ben nods his head and smiles.

They fish in silence.

Suddenly Ben points and yells, 'Look!'

An albatross glides low over the skin of the ocean. The span of its barely moving wings are more than twice Ben's height.

'How does he do it?' Ben whispers, more to himself than his father.

They watch as the great bird skims the waves, almost touching, but never touching. Then it disappears.

The little boat rolls in the swell. The sun has gone. A few white caps appear on a leaden sea.

Ben's dad stands and looks around. 'Time to go mate eh? Get your tackle in.'

Ben reels in his lures then draws in the anchor. They stow their equipment and his father starts the engine and points the nose in the direction of the distant coast.

'What time does the co-op shut, Dad?'

His father laughs. 'Good idea, mate. It'll be our secret.'

'We can still say it's locally caught, can't we? No lie.'

'No lie.'

The tide has turned and is now outgoing, pushed along by a rising wind from the land. The tinny bounces into the waves. Ben's father slows the motor. Ben pulls their spray jackets from under the bow, hands one to his dad and wriggles into his own.

The horizon has disappeared behind an oblique grey curtain. Ben hunkers down in the bow, trying to keep out of the spray and wind. Suddenly they are into the squall. One moment it was far up ahead. Then it is on them. The curtain becomes a wall of water pouring from the sky. Ben's father slows the outboard again. He steers into the swell and white-caps. Ben looks round at him and forces a smile as he hangs onto the side. Water runs down his chin and neck, cold into his jacket and down his chest. The rain gets heavier. It hisses and bounces off the dark ocean skin and rattles on the bow of the tinny.

His fathers peers into the driving rain. Water is up to their ankles. Ben grabs the anchor bucket and starts bailing. He can hardly see. Water is all around them, under the boat, above the boat. In the boat and creeping higher.

Suddenly a huge, rolling white-maned wave appears from nowhere, engulfs them, and is gone. The boat is full of water and sinking.

Ben's father yells, and beckons him to the stern. He hands over the tiller then splashes through the water on his hands and knees to the centre of the boat.

Ben watches him frantically bailing. Bucketful after bucketful goes over the side but the water level doesn't fall. The rain belts down as though intent on killing them.

Eventually it eases. His father keeps bailing. The water level drops.

They swap places again and Ben bails with aching arms until only a few centimetres of water remain swishing from one end to the other as the boat rises and falls.

'Ya all right?' his dad yells.

Ben gives him thumbs up and smiles. At least he hopes he smiles. He's not sure whether he can make his face do what his mind doesn't want.

His father has one hand on his shirt pocket, the one with the phone in it. Should he call for help? They are no longer in danger of sinking. They are heading for the bar, the rain is easing. Ben is coping. A good kid. Doesn't panic. Didn't really want to be here. But has handled it well.

Suddenly they are hit by another huge wave. The boat twists into the swell. The nose goes under. Man and boy are in the water. Under the water. Ben thinks he is never going to come up.

He surfaces gasping and blinded, looking for his father, trying to find something to grab on the upturned tinny, fighting panic and more frightened than he has ever been in his life.

Moments later, his father's head burst from the water next to him, wild eyed and spluttering. He reaches out to Ben and grasps him by the shoulder. 'Ya all right?' he yells.

Ben is so scared he can't speak. He jerks his head up and down in a yes.

'We'll try to right it,' his father shouts.

They take hold of the gunwale and rhythmically rock the boat, pushing and pulling in unison. But the weight of the outboard and the resistance of the water are too much. They give up. Ben's father edges his way to the stern and climbs onto the hull. He reaches down and pulls Ben up next to him. They crouch, facing each other, coughing and choking as they straddle the upturned boat like it's a dead whale.

His father shakes his head in shock and disbelief. 'Whada bugger. Jeeeesuz.' Still coughing, he unzips his waterproofs and slides his hand to his shirt pocket and his phone.

It is not there.

Somewhere below it is sinking in fifty metres of water. He can see the look of dismay on Ben's face. He fights back panic and searches for words of comfort for Ben. Their life jackets will keep them afloat. In the bow are emergency flares and a beacon. Angie will realise something is wrong when they don't contact her. She'll sound the alarm. They just have to keep calm, and wait.

He explains all this to Ben and tells him he is going to dive into the boat for the flares and beacon. Ben nods, without speaking. His face is white under his tan, his mouth is open like a fish out of water. His father draws him closer. Hugs him. Why did he do it? Should've stayed in the river. He takes the line from the bow and loops it around Ben's chest. He slides off the hull, takes a deep breath, bobs under the water and is gone.

Ben concentrates on what his father will be doing. There will be plenty of air trapped underneath. It will be dark, but not hard to find the bow locker where the emergency equipment is. Then he'll come back out. They'll set off the flare. Activate the beacon. Someone will see them and come to the rescue.

He waits.

He taps on the hull of the tinny.

There is no response.

He taps again. Nothing.

Ben panics. He pounds the hull of the boat and screams, 'Dad! Dad! Dad!'

His father's head bursts from the water half a metre away, triumphantly holding the flares and beacon. He fixes the beacon onto the boat. It winks rhythmically. When he has recovered his breath, he activates the flare and holds it high above his head. Ben thinks of the Statue of Liberty and a promised holiday in New York when he is fifteen. The flare fizzes. A miniature red space rocket hisses into the grey sky, it reaches its zenith, hangs for a moment before curving and dropping towards earth. The world is silent once more except for the drum of rain and the slap of water.

Ben's father ties the other end of the line around his own chest. They brace their outstretched arms on the upturned hull for support. The rain eases, then stops. The sky is blue again. The sun shines low in the horizon.

Ben's father is horrified at what he has done. A victim of stupid pride, wanting to catch a fish to impress his son, to impress his wife, to show what a smart dad he is.

He struggles to find words for Ben. 'Someone'll see the flare. They're visible for miles,' he tells him.

Ben nods. He is cold. The two of them rise and fall on the swell with the upturned boat. At each peak they see the pale thread of coastline where the surf is breaking. The sun sinks lower.

'What if no one comes, Dad?'

His father has been silently asking himself the same question. It'll be a few hours yet before Angie begins to worry. Longer again before worry turns to alarm and she contacts police and the coastguard. By then it will be night, and moonless. They are a black speck in a black ocean.

'Someone will.'

'What if they don't?'

'Your mum'll raise the alarm. People get rescued all the time. You read about it everyday.'

Ben tries to blink water from his eyes. 'I'm cold.'

'Keep moving a bit.'

'What about sharks, Dad?'

'They're attracted by blood. There's none here.'

'Good thing we didn't catch anything then,' Ben says.

'Yeah.' His father forces a laugh.

A seagull lands close by, examines them through gold-ringed eyes, decides there is no food, and leaves.

Ben is angry at its indifference. He thinks how easy for a bird. In no time at all it will be on land, squawking and fighting with the other gulls for picnickers' chips in the park.

The gulls are indifferent. The sea is indifferent. Nothing and no one cares about them.

Ben looks across as his father, who forces a smile.

At that moment, both realise that the upturned tinny is lower in the water. Suddenly it starts to sink fast. The line that secured them safely to the bow is dragging them under. They are pulled down and drawn like lures through the water into the depth. Ben's father hacks at the line, cuts it free of the bow, kicks for the surface pulling Ben behind him as the boy thrashes legs and arms, lungs bursting. Drowning.

They are on the surface, gulping air, still alive, coughing and choking, salt-wave-slapped and full of fear. They hang boatless, legs dangling in the water, two humans in a vast ocean.

Ben's father grasps him by the shoulders and looks into his white face. 'It's OK. We'll be all right.'

Ben nods and takes his father's hands.

'Are you up for a long swim? Just in case someone doesn't come,' his dad asks.

Ben nods. 'Yeah,' he manages to say, 'I wish I had my boogie board with me.'

'We'll just take our time. If we get picked up, well and good. If not, we'll make it under our own steam.'

They set off, tied together with a long line. Both know how quickly people can be separated in the water. You are with mates one minute, they have disappeared out of sight in the swell the next. But it is difficult swimming tied to someone; one arm catches the line with each downward sweep. They keep going, regularly raising their heads to sight land, a thin line on the horizon that appears and disappears as the out-coming swell rolls by.

After what seems forever, Ben's father stops.

'What's wrong?' Ben asks as he draws alongside.

'Nothing. You OK?'

'We're not getting far.'

'Yes we are. It's slow. But we're getting there.'

Ben thinks of his aching arms. 'We don't seem any closer than when we started.' Ben tries to hide his dismay.

'The tide's against us, but we'll take our time. Don't try to rush things.'

Ben is tired. So is his father, but neither wants to show it.

They rest, treading water, rising and falling with the rhythm of the swell.

As they lift to a peak, Ben points towards land and yells. 'Something's coming!'

'Where?'

'There, that flashing yellow light,' Ben shouts again and points.

'You're right,' his father yells.

'It's a boat,' Ben tells him. In a moment, his fear and exhaustion are gone. 'They saw the flare.' He grins at his father.

They hang in the water, watch and wait, almost overwhelmed by relief.

But the light comes no closer. No matter how intently they look at it, the light only blinks in the gloom but doesn't move.

'It's not a boat.'

'Of course it is. It has to be,' Ben insists.

'Then why doesn't it get closer?'

Ben has no answer.

His father finally realises. 'It's a buoy. The light's just come on.'

They tread water and watch, the horrible truth sinking in.

'Come on, son.' His father starts swimming towards the winking light. He is almost towing Ben.

The buoy is yellow, the size of the exercise ball that Angie uses. An aerial points skyward; on its tip is the flashing light they have been watching. There is a narrow fender around the middle at water level. Below that, it is crusted in small black mussels. Ben grabs a handle on one side and his father one on the other.

'It's a wave buoy. Measures the swell,' his father explains.

He looks in the direction of land, faint and low on the horizon. To the south, a lighthouse flashes its warning. The first hint of evening colour is in the sky. It's still a long swim to safety. He looks at Ben. His son is shivering. He is hanging tight onto the buoy, his forehead resting on the back of his hands. His father unties the line that joins them, loops it through the two handles then reties it so they are both attached.

'You're supposed to sing in times like this,' his father says.

'Uh?' Ben looks at him as though he is mad.

'Keeps your spirits up. That's what they did in the war and stuff. Do you feel like singing?'

Ben shakes his head, 'No way.'

'Me neither.' His father tries to think of what to say, something that will take their minds off things, something encouraging, uplifting. He doesn't want to keep thinking of his own stupidity.

What kept other people alive while they waited to be rescued? Did they think of hot barbecued sausages? Warmth? Family and friends? The moment when a rescue boat would pick them up? God?

He looks at Ben. Ben is shivering. Hanging tight onto the buoy, head bowed.

'Ben.'

His son looks up.

'This is what we're gonna do. I'm going for help. You're staying here. I…'

'No!' Ben yells.

'Let me finish, son. I'll tie you on. The life jacket'll keep you afloat as well. You've got enough clothes on to stop ya freezing. You'll be cold, but all right. Like a winter night in bed without a doona.'

'What if ya don't come back!'

'Of course I'll come back.'

'I'll come with you.'

'You're too tired.'

'I'm not. I can swim as good as you.'

'Ben. this way's best. We might even be back in time for the party. What a story you'll have to tell, eh.'

'No!'

Ben's father unties the line from around his waist.

'Don't, Dad. Don't leave me.'

His father loops the line through the handle that Ben is clinging to and secures it to his son.

'You can't.' Ben weeps.

His father holds him tight. He hands him his knife. 'You'll be OK. Trust me. I'll be back. Soon. Hang on.'

Ben lunges at his father, who twists away and pushes clear of the buoy. He swims a few strokes. Turns. He lifts his arm to Ben in a farewell, then begins to swim towards land. Ben watches him disappear in the troughs of the swell.

Venus, the brilliant evening star, rises in the west as the sun disappears below the horizon. Ben thinks, what if it is a plane coming to rescue him, to lift him from the water, then find his swimming father and fly them to the barbecue, where everyone would gather around as he told his story.

Whenever he sees Venus, he hears the voice of his mother telling him that it's actually a planet, not a star, and after the sun and moon, is the brightest body in the sky. It comforts him to see it shining there. Maybe his mum's looking at it too.

How far will his father have swum by now? Will he reach land before dark? Will he try to swim over the bar and into the river? Or will he pick the surf beach?

Sharks like to attack at sunset. Ben thinks of his legs and feet dangling below in the water. Involuntarily, he draws up his knees closer to his chest and they rub against the mussel-encrusted buoy.

He is cold. His hands hurt. The line around his chest is too tight.

Ben tries to think of other things: his father swimming steadily towards land; his mum waiting; the cake she's baked – chocolate; Alex and Luke arriving for the barbecue; his new boogie board. Maybe a rescue boat already on its way. Will it find him in the dark? Will it see his father?

Above his head, the buoy flashes its signal, over and over and over.

Ben closes his salt-swollen eyelids to keep out the light. He is so cold, cold in his belly, cold in his bones. What if he dies tied to the buoy and sharks come and tear his legs off? What if they come before he dies, black fins circling? Hurtling in, big mouths and chainsaw teeth ripping and pulling at his flesh.

Ben sobs uncontrollably. He chokes on his own tears and the ocean that forever slaps at him. Eventually he has no tears left, only salt water from the sea. He tugs at the strings of small black mussels that are growing beneath the water line and breaks some free. From his pocket he takes his father's knife and tries to pry one open. His hands are too cold and he can't force the blade between the lips. He tries repeatedly and fails. The mussels fall from his clumsy hands. Eventually he breaks one open by holding it on the edge of the narrow fender and hitting it with the knife handle. He pulls at the yellow meat and sucks it into his mouth salty and slimy. He gags, then swallows. He breaks open others, slowly and painfully, then eats the insides.

Perhaps he sometimes sleeps for a moment. He doesn't know. The blackness of the night, punctuated only by the measured rhythmic flash of the beacon makes him hallucinate. Venus, now out of sight beneath the horizon, reappears and speeds across the sky. It hovers above, its brilliant light shining down on him like a searchlight. His dad is by his side telling him help is on its way. He has a piece of chocolate cake for him. Then he's gone.

An albatross circles. Its great wings and underbelly are yellow. It appears and disappears in the light of the beacon. It is there. It is gone. It is there. It is gone. It can fly forever. Ben calls out to it. Then the albatross is no more. The beacon flashes in the empty darkness.

Ben tugs at the line to ease the tightness on his chest. He tries to break open more mussels but his hands are too cold and he cuts his fingers. The blood mixes with the water and Ben thinks of blood and sharks. They can smell blood beyond the horizon.

Stars come out in the moonless night and Ben watches as they slowly move across the bowl of the sky.

Why has no one come to rescue him? He listens for the sound of a boat's engine and hears nothing but the sighing of the sea.

He scans darkness for the lights of a rescue helicopter but there is nothing except stars twinkling in the waves.

He believes the albatross returns. It appears on motionless wings and circles. He can see dark eyes looking down on him. Then it is gone.

*

Night passes. Ben hangs from the line tethered to the buoy, rigid with cold, drifting in and out of consciousness or sleep.

First light touches the dark sea. Then dawn. A new day. The sun comes up, brash and red. It is warm on Ben's head. He turns from it and squints towards land through salt-blinded bloodshot eyes. He thinks he can see something moving across the ocean towards him. The albatross again?

He rubs his eyes. Not an albatross. A small boat.

It's moving fast to the north, out to sea. It's not coming to him.

Why hasn't his dad told someone?

Ben can hear the distant roar of the engine. He screams and yells. Fear gives him energy. He drags off his jacket and desperately waves it, a yellow flag above is head. He barely has strength. He struggles to raise his arms. He waves again.

The boat slows. It changes course and heads towards him, bumping over the waves.

Ben's eyes burn in the glare of the sun as the boat narrows the gap. He can make out a solitary figure, a man, standing in the stern, staring in his direction. He watches as the boat gets closer and closer.

The Bathhouse

The travellers were resting after the hot, bumpy journey from the mountains into the city. They sat under an awning on the rooftop of their small hotel, sipping mint tea and watching day pale into dusk as they discussed their adventures. The awning fluttered in the breeze. Swallows flicked through the sky above.

Youssef, their guide, joined them. He grinned, like a kid waiting to be asked, where have you been? What have you been up to? He waited until he had everyone's attention.

I have another story for you, he said. I told you this afternoon how I went to Marrakech to go to school, and I was to live with my aunty, yes?

Everyone remembered, yes.

I told you I was small for my age. Very small. After a few days, I started school. I didn't know anyone and I was shy. Some of the big guys laughed at me and teased me because of my size.

One of the girls kept smiling at me. Maybe she liked me. Maybe she felt sorry for me. I didn't know. So I tried to stand close to her, not for protection, but because I wanted to find out her name. Eventually I heard her friends call her Fatima. It's a nice name. She was really pretty and I wanted to be her friend but was too shy to speak.

Near the end of the first week, my aunty said we would go to the *hammam*, the steam bath. She said 'we'.

We? Together? With the women and the kids? I asked.

That's what I said. Don't they teach you nothing at school?

Youssef looked up at his audience, his eyes wide to emphasise what he was going to say next: males and females don't go to the bathhouse at the same times. Never. Unless they are kids. He gave everyone the now familiar grin that was seldom far from his face.

People take their clothes off in the *hammam*. They are naked. But not men and women together. They go at different times. Then, when kids reach a certain age, if they are boys, they go with the men. If they are girls, they go with the women. Imagine, I was thirteen and my aunty wanted me to go with the women and kids. I'd see her without her clothes! She'd see me without my clothes. Everyone would laugh at me.

Aunty, I'm too old to go to the *hammam* with you. I go with the men, not the women and kids, I told her.

Don't be stupid. You are little, no one will know.

I know. And they will too.

I hadn't yet started to grow pubic hair, but they would still know I wasn't a kid and wonder what I was doing there.

No! I yelled at my aunty.

She hit me across the back of my head. Stupid boy. Yes!

No! I yelled back.

My aunty hit me across the back of my head again. No. I'm your aunty. You do as I tell you. No one is going to notice.

Everybody is going to notice, I shouted again.

Do you think women have nothing better to do than look at a skinny little boy?

I'm not skinny and I'm not a boy, I'm nearly a man, and I'm not going, I told her.

I knew I was skinny, and I knew I was nowhere near being a man, as far as size was concerned. But I still wasn't going to the *hammam* with my aunty and all those old women and girls. Girls! Them with no clothes on. Me with no clothes on. No. A thousand times no.

I ran out of the house and into the street. The women neighbours standing around in the shade talking were old, and ugly. Maybe I shouldn't say that, but I was a boy then, I didn't want to see old women without their clothes.

I wandered the streets hoping somebody would talk to me or that I'd be able to join in a game of football, but nobody took any notice. It was like I was so small I didn't exist. That's what my aunty thought would happen in the *hammam*.

I was thinking all the time of what it was going to be like. I even thought of getting the bus back home to my family. But what would they and and everyone in the village say? They'd all laugh at me. Apart from that, I had no money. And I really, really, wanted to go to school and get an education.

Then I had an idea. As I walked back to my aunty's place, I started pinching and pulling at my cheeks. I knew they would go all bright red, because I'd done it before. They looked pretty amazing. When I was nearly at the house, I bent over a bit and held my belly as though it ached and I had diarrhoea. It's worked at home when I tried to get out of something I didn't want do.

I wobbled into my aunty's house. I leaned against the wall and groaned.

What's the matter? my aunty said.

N-o-thing, I said. I didn't want to overdo it.

She told me to show my tongue. Then she put her hand on my forehead. Sit down. I'll get you a glass of water. Then we'll go to the *hammam*. The steam will sweat it out, she said.

She wasn't as stupid as I thought, in some things anyway.

I sipped the water. I didn't even try pinching my cheeks again or hold my belly or moaning.

She came back a few minutes later with mats and towels and soap and things for the steam bath. Come on, we'll soon have you feeling better, she said, holding out her hand.

She even wanted me to hold her hand, walking down the street like some little kid. I wondered, what was the matter with this woman, my aunty? Maybe she thought if she did that, it really would make me look like a kid.

I shook my head and told her, no, I'm sick.

It will make you better. It was like she was spitting out the words. She didn't seem to believe that people got sick. Not me anyway.

I'm not going, I told her.

You are.

I'm not.

My aunty grabbed me by the ear, pulled me to my feet and marched towards the door. She was a lot bigger than me. I wasn't going to walk to the *hammam* like that. I wriggled free and she grabbed my wrist and held onto my like a crab. There was nothing I could do but go with her.

When we got to the *hammam*, the woman who took the money asked, How old is he?

I thought I was saved.

Yasmin, my aunty said, how old does he look? He's a boy. My nephew.

The woman looked at me again. She looked at my aunty, then let us in. My aunty had saved herself some money.

My aunty took hold of my wrist again and towed me behind her into the change room. It was full of women and kids. My aunty thrust a towel and mat into my hands and said hello to other women. Some of them and the other kids looked at me in a funny way. I hoped they were going to get me kicked out. But no one said anything.

My aunty started to undress, slowly. So did the other women. They talked together but I didn't hear a word they were saying.

I just stood there. I was so scared. I didn't know where to look. But the longer I stood, the worse it got. I couldn't keep my clothes on while everyone else took theirs off.

I started to undress, as slowly as I could. First I took my sandals off and stood holding them for ages.

My aunty glared at me.

I took off my T-shirt.

By that time, all the kids had taken off their clothes and were watching me out of the corner of their eyes because I still hadn't undressed fully. My aunty and the other women were now naked. It was horrible. I didn't know where to look.

There was nothing I could do. So, finally, I took off my shorts. Then my underpants. I stood there with my hands in front of my private parts, wishing I was anywhere in the world but here.

I followed my aunty, the other women and kids from the change room, my head down and my hands covering me. I wanted to die. I wanted to be back in my village. I wanted to be anywhere but here.

As we went into the warm room, a girl screamed. I looked up. It was Fatima from school. She held her hands in front of her belly and I caught a glimpse of dark hair. Then she turned and fled.

I turned and fled the other way towards the exit. I slipped on the wet floor and fell. I skidded on my back across the floor, my legs in the air like a beetle.

I could still hear Fatima screaming hysterically. I grabbed my clothes and ran out of the *hammam*. I ran down the street naked – all the way home, clutching my clothes to me.

Youssef could not stop laughing at the recollection as everyone in the group clapped and roared their appreciation.

After a few minutes, Youssef completed his story. Even now, I still meet people I went to school with who say things like, Youssef, do you remember when you went to the *hammam* with the old women and pretended to be a little boy so you could see Fatima without her clothes?

(With thanks to Khalid Lamlih)

Night Out

My nice clothes. Nicest. Sunday clothes. And lipstick. Check lips. At the mirror, carefully, hand steady no shaking. Shhh. Listen. Shhh. Shhh. Nobody coming. No Mum nobody. Now, shoes. Stockings. Shoes. Shhh. No one. Headscarf. Red. Nice colour, like lipstick. Powder on my nose like Mum. No sneezing. Mirror mirror on the wall.

Going. Go.

Listen.

Wait.

Never never ever. No one. Oooopen the door. Shhh. Slowly. Quite. Quietly. Down the stairs. The stairs. No one. Fairest. Fairest of them all. Stocking feet. Shhhh.

Radio. Mum. Mum listen. Listening. Shh. Tip. Tip. Tip. Tiptoe. Mum. Mum and the radio in the kitchen. Pass the door. Her listening to the man. Careful. Don't want her to hear. Tip toe. The door and the handle. Turn. Turn. Softly. Open door. Softly. Shhh. Close. No noise. Shoes on.

Out!

The street sunshine kids running shouting. Stop. Ohhh. Ohh. Go back? No. Go. Handbag, money, hanky. Which way? This. This way. Quickly. Look back. Door closed. Mum not chasing. Mum listening to the man on the radio.

Me. Alone. Good. Good. Good. People. Cars. Trams. Not good. Go back? No. No. How? Where? Where to find the place for the tram? Walking. Walking.

There! Those people standing. They get on. That's the place. That's it so I follow. Climb on! Sit down, handbag on my knees. Looking out the window. People. Sitting. Coughing.

A man. Money? My purse. Open. There, there's the money.

'Where to, love?'

Smile at him.

'Into town?'

Smile at him.

'You all right, love? Town, is it?'

'Into town?'

Takes my money. Gives some back. And the bit of paper. Ticket. That's it: ticket. Remember that.

It's me. By myself. Doing it. By myself. Into town. Tram rocking stopping starting. Them people coming going on off rocking. That man getting money smiling at me smiling. Me. Looking out the window. No Mum. Me. By myself. Into town. Don't need anybody. Just me. Where's me? It's all everything. So much everything. All. Mum. Where's Mum? With the radio.

Before with her. Holding my hand. Crossing the road. Take care. I can do. I can.

I. I don't know I don't know.

Where is? What name? Where? Think. I remember, think. It is lights lots of people. Waiting. All waiting. Then dark and warm and safe and somewhere. The big woman. Hair. Eyes. Smile. So big up there.

'As far as we go. Everybody off.'

Stopped. The tram's stopped.

'It's where you get off, love.'

Me? Me.

'Do you know where you want to go?'

Everyone going. Me. Me too.

'Your bag. Don't forget it.'

Money. Need money. Got my bag. Thank you. Always say thank you, eh Mum?

'Ta ra. Take care.'

Noise.

Noise.

Noise!

Everyone. Hurry. Standing. Where to how there? Other side of the road. All those people the lights all standing waiting. There! That's it. Careful cross the road. Look and look and look again just like Mum.

So much light my eyes hurt. People talking and waiting and queue slowly we moving past the pictures big pictures beautiful woman. Lovely hair. Soft skin. Not mine. Not mine all dry white rough skin.

Money. They give the woman in the little box money. Bag. Purse. My money, from Mum's jar. Here. Smile. Bit of paper again. Ticket. That's the ticket.

Thank you.

Inside. A lady with a light shows me where. Sit down. Warm. I can do. I can. See me. I can. By myself. Lights off. Dark. All these people. Sitting watching. Can hardly see anyone. Now. That's it, the pictures show lovely lady up there. Lovely hair. Not mine lovely skin not mine man kissing her. Kissing kissing not me her. Not me. Everyone watching. Looking up watching. The pictures. All that lovely lovely colour.

Whisper 'Do you want a toffee?'

Not the pictures but.

Me?

'Butterscotch.'

Thank you. Nice. Sweet butterscotch. Nice man next to me. Always say thank you.

The man is angry. Up there that one not this one.

Ohhh no. Shooting her not me. Hurting ohhh her not me. Ohhh no. The man up there running running.

'Have another butterscotch.'

Nice man.

Holding my hand.

Thank. You. Sweet butterscotch. Suck don't crunch. Mum! See me by myself not you just me.

The man up there is gone, hiding in the dark he's been bad.

Holding my hand. This man. Here. Tighter.

Hurt. You are hurting. No don't do. No. Mum said. Never let anyone.

Don't do.

Mum!

Mum!

Butterscotch man is gone. Dropped his butterscotch.

The woman with the light. Shining on me. 'All right? You all right dear?'

Light. In my eyes. Mmmm. All right.

'Good. Shush then. Please.'

Spit out onto the floor the butterscotch.

Man up there has been bad. Trouble. In trouble. Now he's gone. Everyone up there has gone. Everyone down here gone. Just me. Time for me too. Got my bag butterscotch cracks when I step on it sticks to my shoe.

Outside, the road. No sun now. Dark in the sky. No stars. Bright lights hurt my eyes. People people people cars. Trams. Which. Which. Mum! Mum! Which one? Don't know. Ohh Mum!

Standing. Looking at all the people everything. The trams. Which way? Tram gone. Butterscotch on my shoe. Scrape. Scrape. Hate butterscotch. Don't know. Don't know. Why did? I don't.

Can't.

Mum!

People looking.

Not me shouting.

Mum says don't shout. Me. Standing. People pushing stop it. Don't. Don't touch me. Hurry hurry hurrying away. My heart, pupp-pupp, pupp-pupp, pupp-pupping, under my coat were it's warm. Along the street getting away.

Quiet now, no people. Dark. A dog, little dog. Come here doggy. Come. Come here. I won't hurt.

Gone dog. Gone. Dark. Dark on shiny street.

No one. Me. No dog. No one. Just me. No people. No butterscotch. No man. Big big gate. Dark behind. Not in the dark. Mum says that. Not in the…

Mum! Mum! Which way? Back. Back back back.

People again.

The pictures again. Big pictures beautiful woman. Lights going now. Off. Another off. All off. No lights on beautiful woman.

Home now.

Home. Where?

How?

How?

Then. Then. There's the tram man. Ticket man.

Ticket man on the tram.. Waving. That one, waving. That one. Standing on the tram. At the door.

'Hello again. D'y have a good time?'

To me. Me.

There was a bad man. Up there. The pictures.

'Long as ya enjoyed yourself, love.'

Rattle up the road shaking rolling. People squashing me. People. Sitting. Standing. Smelling face stuff. Powder like mine, and beer stuff cigarettes. Talking. Talking laughing shouting.

Hand hurts. Butterscotch-sticky dress.

Where? Am I? Nearly no one now. Stops. Everyone gone.

Me. Just me.

'End of the line, love. It's where ya got on 'n' where ya get off. Ya can't sleep on the tram, can ya?' Smiles. 'Somebody meeting you? Ta ra.'

Tram gone. People gone. The road. No people. No pushing. No noise.

Which way?

Down. Down the hill. Hurting feet. Keep on. Mum will be pleased. I done it. Me. Me. Just me.

Empty road. Under the lights. No trams. No cars. Nobody.

Singing man singing. Down the road. Towards me. Singing. Shouting. Bad. Shouldn't. Not that word. Nearer. Nearer.

'Where ya goin, girl?'

Man stops. Falls. Help him. Help him. Shouts. At me. 'Wharrrayer!'

Hurry run.

Quiet now. Walking. Walking. Where am? Where? What? Oh. Oh. Where. No one under the lights. Cat. A cat. Cheee-cheee, cheee-cheee. Lovely cat. Cheee-cheee. Come come come lovely cat. Soft. Mum said no can't have. No no no never.

Mum. Soon. Home. Mum! Me. Look me. Clever. By myself. The pictures. Beautiful woman beautiful skin. beautiful hair not like me not like me. There. There my door open my house my light. Inside. Mum. Mum. There's Mum coming. To me. Smile for Mum. Hello Mum.

Mum running to me.

No Mum! No! My hair let go let go! Mum no!

'Where were ya? Ah told ya never! Been off mi head! Worried sick!'

No Mum don't hit. Let go my hair. Mum's hand hard in my face. Hurt hurt hurt.

Stop! No Mum

'I told ya. Never! How many times ah told ya? Never out alone! 'Do ya hear mi? How many times? How many times ah told ya? Never never!'

But Mum! No Mum!

No no no Mum. Not the belt Mum no no.

Swish swish on my back legs arms bottom swish swish crack crack swish crack ohh, ohh, hurts hurts hurts.

No Mum. I by myself.

'Police been looking for ya!'

Smack bang crack.

Don't don't why Mum? Don't.

'I told ya never ever by yourself outa my brain I am!'

Crack whack.

Don't! Please.

Hurts hurts me.

On the floor now. Mum getting me up whack again fist in my face my head my hands blood on my hands to my nose. Mum please no why? Why?

Cry cry crying. Stop stop. Let me up up.

Mum down kneeling holding me crying squeezing hugging touching hurting wiping my face the blood on her skirt.

Mum? Muuum?'

'You been hours. Hours. Did something happen to ya? Ya all right? Never ever! Never ever again! You hear me? You hear me? Never ever! Never ever!'

Never Mum. Never.

The Devil You Know

The Woman climbed the hill in the fading light. She reached a walnut tree. She stopped and sat beneath the tree's long shadow and looked back down over the wide stony river in the valley below. Houses clung to the steep slopes where the river narrowed and flowed through the village. Fruit trees and corn grew in patches of rich soil between low dry-stone walls.

The Woman could hear the distant sound of children playing, an occasional car or motorbike, the bleating of goats and the bad tempered braying of a donkey. She came here at the end of each day to marvel at the world.

After a while, she heard the rattle of stones on the steep, dusty donkey track behind her. A man stopped as he drew level. He bade her good day and asked if he could sit on a close-by rock and rest.

The man was a stranger to the district but there was nothing in his demeanour to arouse her fears so the Woman nodded and said, 'Yes.'

The man lowered himself onto the rock and laid his staff on the ground beside him. Although he had come down the barren, rocky path where people had crossed the mountain for thousands of years he appeared to be neither begrimed nor tired.

He asked if she lived in the village.

She told him, 'All my life.'

He asked, 'Tell me, what are the people like?'

'Like people everywhere.'

The man laughed.

'Why do you laugh?' the Woman asked the stranger.

'Are they good or bad?' the man persisted.

'Sometimes good. Sometimes bad.'

'That is because they are what I make them. If they are not bad, I can make them bad,' he told her.

It was now the Woman's turn to laugh. 'How? How can you do such a thing?'

Without turning to look at her, the man said, 'Because I am the Devil.'

The Woman had never met the Devil before. She had met *djinni*, and like everyone else, she knew of Aladdin, and Aisha Qandisha, the beautiful seductive woman with the legs of a goat, who lives in riverbeds and flames. She was afraid of none of them. But the Devil himself?

'How do I know you are the Devil?' she asked, looking at him nervously from the corners of her eyes. He seemed a normal enough man.

'I will prove it to you. I will show you how bad I can make people.' The man who said he was the Devil got up from the stone and collected his staff. 'We will meet here in one week. By then you will have seen the terrible things people have done because of me.' He set off down the path to the village without speaking further.

*

The richest man in the village was Said Benjelloun. His wife Nada was the most beautiful woman in the whole valley. Said and Nada loved each other. They lived in the largest house for kilometres around. Said Benjelloun had the most apple trees, the most walnut trees, the most goats, and the largest amount of land. Said Benjelloun and Nada were very happy. Next spring, Nada was to give birth to their first child.

The Devil wasted no time in putting his plan into action. That night while the couple were sleeping, the Devil crept into their room and whispered into Said Benjelloun's ear. He told him his wife had betrayed him and the child she was carrying was not his. He said that Nada planned to murder him as he slept so she could marry the child's father, a rich local merchant. She would then blame his death on a thief. The Devil instructed Said Benjelloun to hide a knife under his pillow to defend himself.

The Devil then walked silently to the other side of the bed, leaned over and whispered in Nada's ear. He told her that the husband she loved was convinced she had been unfaithful and that the child she carried belonged to another. That night her husband would kill her as she slept, blaming the murder on a thief.

When they awoke the following morning, each remembered their dream. The love and trust that had been with them since their betrothal many years before was now replaced by suspicion and fear. They each concealed their feelings and went about their daily business.

That night, Said Benjelloun slipped alone into the bed chamber and concealed a dagger beneath his pillow.

When his back was turned as the couple prepared to retire for the night, Nada slid her hand beneath Said Benjelloun's pillow. Her fingers touched the cold steel of the dagger, confirming her dream. She was about to be murdered by her husband.

They lay, side by side, filled no longer with love but with hate and fear. Each prepared to strike. They remained like that the long night.

When cock crow heralded the dawn, Said Benjelloun was sure this was the moment his wife would strike. He slid his dagger from beneath the pillow.

Feeling the movement of her husband, Nada unsheathed the blade she had concealed amongst her clothes, flung herself on him and plunged the steel into his breast.

Said Benjelloun, with a last dying effort, thrust his dagger deep into his wife's belly.

*

One week later, the Woman was once more sitting on the rock under the walnut tree after climbing the long path from the village. She looked down on the valley and thought of the terrible thing that had happened to Said Benjelloun and his beautiful wife Nada.

After a while, a man came down the path behind her and stopped when he drew level. He bade her good day. He asked if he could sit on the near by rock.

'Yes,' the Woman said. She did not turn to look at him. She knew who he was.

'Well?' said the Devil after some moments. 'What do you think of the things I made Said Benjelloun and his wife Nada do?'

'That was nothing to do with you. People do not need the Devil to instruct them how to be bad. For seven days I will seek out the terrible things they do without you.' The Woman stood. 'We will meet here again.' She set off back down the mountain to the valley floor and the village.

*

Seven days later, as agreed, the Woman climbed from the valley. It was evening. The sun was setting beyond the mountain. The land below was already in dark shadow.

The Woman was weary. She had been on a long and perilous journey. She stopped frequently to rest. Had anyone been close to her on the mountain path, they would have noticed that her face was grey and haggard, and her mouth was no more than a thin tight line between chin and nose.

She reached the walnut tree and stopped. She lowered her body and sat beneath the dark branches and looked down on the wide stony river in the valley. She could hear distant sounds, children playing, an occasional car or motorbike, the bleating of goats. A donkey.

After a while, she heard the rattle of stones. A man came down the path behind her and stopped when he drew level. He bade her good day and asked if he could sit on the rock and rest next to her. She nodded without turning. She knew who he was.

The Devil sat in silence. Eventually he said, 'Well? Tell me.' He laughed, confident of his superiority.

The Woman began to speak. 'In the village lives my oldest friend. Her name is Latifa. I went to visit her. The house was in darkness. I knocked on the door. Eventually she opened it. She was weeping.

'Latifa told me that her two sons and husband had drowned. They were taking a boatload of people to another country under cover of darkness. The pay was good. The boat sank and everyone on board died. My friend closed the door and I went away.

'In the village market I came across a group of women keening. I asked what was the source of their grief. One turned to me and said they had been forced to leave their homes farther down the valley because the King had diverted the river which irrigated their fields. Now all the water went to the green lawns and gardens of his palace and their orchards had died. Their once-productive fields were dust and stone. They no longer had food for their children and themselves.

'I wandered through the market until I came upon a group of men arguing angrily among themselves. Each said their god was the only god and only those who followed their god would find paradise. The argument became more intense. They started to strike each other with their fists, then with sticks, then with stones, then with knives. I fled.

'Farther down the valley I came across a long convoy of trucks each one packed with women. They were tied together like animals, standing, shoulder to shoulder in the heat, each prevented from falling only by the person next to them. The air was thick with dust which descended on them like a grey shroud. Each truck was followed by a vehicle on which was mounted a machine gun manned by a grim-faced soldier. I stood and watched as the convoy passed. The women silently implored me with their eyes, or held out their hands, for water, or liberation I knew not which.

'Eventually the trucks disappeared into the folds of the mountain and I was left alone by the side of the road. I too was now garbed with a shroud of grey dust.

'I put the mountains behind me and descended to a city on the plains thinking to find someone in authority to whom I could report the terrible things that were happening. For many hours, I walked under the hot, white dome of the sky, alongside the high walls of the king's palace. As I passed the guarded gates, I glimpsed green lawns, trees, and sparkling fountains inside the vast grounds.

'Many wide roads converged on the city. When I arrived, I stopped people and implored them to tell me where I might go so my grievances could be related to authorities and the terrible things I had seen brought to an end and to justice. Each one pointed in a different direction until I became confused. I walked wide boulevards between tall buildings. I traversed narrow lanes and markets, always asking. I was told to go back the way I had come to find the answers. I was told the place I sought was around the next corner or that I had already past it. Or that no such place existed.

'Weary and dispirited, I turned my back on the city on the plains. I walked for many hours and saw no one. I stopped to rest when I gained the crest of a ridge and turned to look back over the long path I had traversed.

'Far away, pillars of smoke blacker than the blackest night, reached into the sky above the city. As each column climbed higher and higher, another sprouted below it and ascended, joining in a massive, impenetrable blanket that spread and drifted and engulfed the whole horizon. Black lines of people crawled like ants from the burning city, converged and swept as one in the direction of the ocean.

'I felt like I was standing on a rock overhanging a valley and that any moment I would fall onto the boulders far below.

'I withdrew and retraced my steps whence I had come, back into the mountains.

'In the village where I had earlier passed the group of quarrelling men, the market was a smouldering ruin. Stalls were still burning and flames danced with their own reflections in crimson pools. Women, children and men were weeping among the smoking debris.'

By the time she finished telling the Devil her story, the rays of the morning sun were spilling over the sharp peaks of the mountain.

She turned. The stone on which the Devil had sat was empty. She searched around the base of the rock for footprints or other signs of his presence. There were none. Had she proved to him that what he believed to be his bad deeds were actually the works of people? That he'd had nothing to do with any of them?

The woman rose and slowly made her way down the stony path, towards the silent village.